SERGEANT'S SECRET BABY

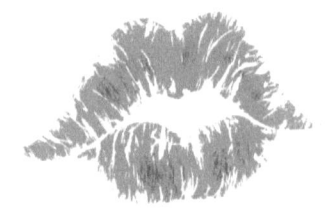

EVERNIGHT PUBLISHING ®

www.evernightpublishing.com

Copyright© 2022

Paige Warren

Editor: Audrey Bobak

Cover Art: Jay Aheer

ISBN: 978-0-3695-0624-5

SERGEANT'S SECRET BABY

DEDICATION

This one is for my readers! Your support means so much
to me.

SERGEANT'S SECRET BABY

SERGEANT'S SECRET BABY

Paige Warren

Copyright © 2017

Chapter One

Shiloh Anderson threw back another shot and then grimaced as the whiskey went down, leaving a burn in its wake. It was not her drink of choice, but if she was stuck in this godforsaken place, she might as well make it bearable. Her shit of a boyfriend—make that *ex*-boyfriend—had left her stranded in the middle of BFE. Not that she had a home anymore. The asshat had not only left her here, but he'd taken off with all of her crap in the back of his truck. The dick hadn't even left her a change of clothes or her cell phone charger. Thank God she had her purse.

The black screen of her iPhone mocked her, the damn thing having died the hour before. It didn't matter though. There was no one for her to call. Her entire family had written her off as a screw-up and waste of space. The few friends she'd had were long gone, thanks to the mistake she'd been dating the past year. She should have never stayed with him, especially after the first time she found out about his cheating ways. Despite their rocky relationship, she'd agreed to move across country with him for a fresh start. He'd promised things would be better when they reached South Carolina, where his family was supposedly waiting for them.

Shiloh motioned to the bartender for another shot. She'd have to be blind not to notice his swagger and the impressive ink covering his massive arms. Lickable. Definitely lickable. Maybe he'd be up for a one-night stand and let her crash at his place until morning. She doubted anything would look any better in the light of day, but at least it would buy her some time. Thank the Lord she hadn't agreed to a joint bank account. The asshat probably would have cleaned her out. As it was, she had enough to survive for a short while, but not enough to rent a place and start fresh. If she hadn't funded part of their trip and his truck repairs, then she'd have a few thousand more in the account.

The bartender crossed his arms over his massive chest. "I think you've had enough for the night. Why don't you let me call you a cab?"

She didn't want a cab. She wanted another drink.

"Glaring at me through blurry eyes isn't the answer," the bartender said. "Look, where's the guy you came with? Shouldn't he be back by now?"

"He's not coming back."

Dark eyebrows rose into the hair falling over his forehead. "What do you mean he's not coming back? Are you trying to tell me you're stranded here?"

"That about sums it up." She tapped the bar. "Now, how about that drink?"

"Sweetheart, I don't think your problems are going to be solved at the bottom of a bottle. What you need is a place to sleep. I know I'm a complete stranger, and you have no reason to trust me, but I own this place and live in the apartment upstairs. I share the place with my brother, but I can crash at a friend's house tonight and let you have my room."

"You don't have to do that," she mumbled, dropping her gaze. "I'll figure things out."

"Uh-huh. You've been sitting here for hours. How's that working out for you?"

She shrugged.

"My name's Dallas Edwards. I've lived in this town my entire life, and anyone here can vouch for me. I promise, if you stay at my apartment tonight, you'll be safe, and I won't expect anything in return." He smiled a little. "I have a soft spot for damsels in distress. It's how I ended up with my fiancée."

"You go around offering your bed to every woman who walks through the door?"

He laughed. "No, and Rebecca would have my balls if I did. However, I think she'd understand just this once. Look, my brother is probably going to be out all night. It's his last night before being shipped overseas. You'll have the place to yourself."

"All right, but only because I'm desperate and sleeping in the parking lot doesn't sound like much fun."

"The stairs are around the side of the bar." He reached under the bar and pulled out a keyring with just one key on it. "This is my spare. You can use it to let yourself in. There is some cheese and yogurt in the fridge or some crackers in the cabinet. If you'd like, I can have the kitchen make you a burger to take up with you."

Her stomach rolled. "I don't think I can handle food right now."

"If you need something to sleep in, I keep my shirts in the second drawer of the dresser. I'll bring Rebecca with me in the morning. Maybe she'll have a change of clothes for you." His gaze scanned her. "Size six?"

"Eight."

"Go get some sleep."

She accepted the key. "I'm Shiloh Anderson, and you should know that crap like this seems to happen to me all the time. I appreciate having a place to crash for the night, though."

"If you need anything, I'll be down here another three hours."

She held up her phone. "I don't suppose you have an iPhone charger, do you?"

"Sorry. Which model? I'll see if I can find something at the store for you on my way over tomorrow."

"The newest one. My jerk of an ex has my charger and all of my stuff is in his truck, probably halfway to South Carolina by now."

He nodded. "Go get some rest, Shiloh. I promise things won't look so horrible in the morning. And at least you were stranded in Gulch Springs. We're a friendly place, and we like to help out when we can. You might decide you want to stick around."

She wasn't so sure about that, but she supposed one place was just as good as another. Shiloh thanked him again, slid off her barstool, and stumbled her way outside and up the stairs. It took her three tries to get the key in the lock and to open the door. Shutting it firmly, she twisted the bolt and staggered down the hall. There were three doors. One was open, and she thanked God she'd found a bathroom. After taking care of her needs, she stared at the other two doors. Dallas hadn't said which one was his, but if his brother was going to be out all night, did it really matter?

Shiloh pushed open the door to the first bedroom. She flicked on the switch, winced at the bright light, and immediately shut it off. Stripping out of her boots and clothes, she face planted on the bed, bare-assed as the day she was born. After a bit of wiggling, she managed to pull the covers over her and curled up in the center of the queen-size bed. It had been a long time since she'd had a bed to herself. Maybe if she weren't completely plastered, she'd have enjoyed it a bit more. Of course, now that jerkwad was out of her life, she was going to have tons of time to sleep by herself.

The alcohol-induced haze made her feel like she was floating, drifting on a cloud. Her stomach no longer felt queasy. Shiloh closed her eyes and dozed. A while later, she thought she heard a noise in the room, but dismissed it as her imagination. Dallas had said she'd probably have the place to herself. And she'd remembered to lock the door. She sighed and rolled over. When the bed dipped, she bolted upright, clutching the blankets to her chest.

"Hello?" She tried to see in the inky darkness, but could only make out the shape of a man. Oh hell, had she picked the wrong bed?

There was a click and a lamp turned on. She squinted until her eyes adjusted. The man sitting beside her was even larger than his brother, and she hadn't thought that was physically possible. Dark hair was buzzed short, and his profile showed a strong jaw and long, straight nose. There was an Army tattoo on one bicep. His broad back was toned, and his arms looked large enough to break someone in half. *Or cuddle them really close.* She gave herself a mental slap. When his blue eyes focused on her, her tongue stuck to the roof of her mouth. No one had ever looked at her like that before.

"Looks like my brother got me a going-away present after all." Appreciation lit his eyes as he scanned her.

She shook her head.

"No? Well, sweetheart, I can't think of any other

reason for a naked woman to be in my bed."

"I picked the wrong room," she mumbled.

He gave her a sardonic smile. "I know for a fact Rebecca wouldn't approve of Dallas sharing his room with any naked women except her. So, if you were looking to trap him in some way, you picked the wrong mark."

"No, I … he's helping me."

The man turned and braced his hands on either side of her hips, leaning in close, his lips nearly brushing hers. "What I think is that your plan isn't going the way you'd thought it would so you're making up stories. But I'm a pretty nice guy. I'll give you thirty seconds to get that sweet ass of yours out of my bed, dressed, and the fuck out of this apartment."

She licked her lips and didn't move.

"Or, if you're still here in thirty seconds, I'm going to take it as an invitation and see if those lips taste as sweet as they look."

Her eyes widened. He wouldn't really kiss her, would he? She trembled a little at the thought of the powerful man caging her in putting his lips on hers. The thought of his hands on her body… Heat flushed her cheeks and spread down into her chest. She wasn't seriously considering sitting here just to see if he'd really do it, was she?

"Time's up."

Her lips parted, but before she could utter a word of protest, his mouth pressed against hers, his tongue invading and tasting. Oh Lord! Shiloh had never been kissed so thoroughly before. His expertise was enough to make her weak-kneed and ready to beg for more. Her body burned and she dropped the blankets to reach for him. As he pushed her back against the bed, she became acutely aware of the fact he was just as naked as her.

Was she really about to have sex with a complete stranger? She didn't even know his name!

He trailed hot kisses down her neck, giving her ear a nip. A shiver skated down her spine as her nipples puckered. *Oh, hell yeah! He can do whatever he wants to me.*

His hands burned her as they skimmed her heated flesh. The blankets were kicked out of the way as they lay hip to hip. Shiloh gasped and arched against him as his lips closed over her nipple, drawing on it long and hard. Her nails scored his shoulders as the devil inside urged her to take whatever she wanted, what she needed. It had been so long since she'd felt desired, and never had anyone ever made her body sing like this nameless man did.

His cock brushed the inside of her thigh as she spread her legs to accommodate him. Shiloh was eager and ready, but her mystery lover seemed to have other ideas. He claimed her lips again, kissing her like she was the best present he'd ever received. It almost seemed like he expected this to be the last kiss he'd ever experience and he wanted to make it count. Shiloh ran her foot up and down his calf, hoping to encourage him to take things a little further. She wanted him, and she didn't want to wait.

"What do you want, beautiful?" he asked, his breath teasing her ear.

"I want to feel you inside of me."

He moved away from her and she heard a drawer open and the rip of a packet. He'd left her in a dreamy haze, and she floated, blissfully, as she waited for him to return. His body covered hers, and she felt his cock brush against her, the latex of the condom cool against her skin.

"Better brace yourself, angel."

She wrapped her hands around his bulging biceps

as he thrust forward, sinking balls deep inside of her. Shiloh moaned and wrapped her legs around his waist, never wanting to let him go. He felt so incredible, so right, so fucking perfect. She didn't think it could get any better, but then he moved, his cock driving deep and hard. His hands slid under her back and gripped her shoulders, pulling down toward every thrust as he pounded into her.

Shiloh cried out in ecstasy, her body coming undone beneath him, flying to heights she never felt before. Her climax seemed to go on forever, making her toes curl and her breath catch. The powerful man over her groaned and stilled against her, his cock pulsing inside of her. She stroked his back as her body relaxed. Between the alcohol and the incredible sex, she was suddenly ready to sleep and could feel herself drifting.

Her eyes slid shut, and she felt her breathing even out. As she spiraled into oblivion, she felt him pull out and heard a muffled curse. Too tired to care, she snuggled deeper into the bed and fell asleep.

****

Drake had no idea who the angel in his bed was, but he did know one thing. He was in deep shit. Not because her body had been sweet and willing, or because the feel of her hands on him had made him want things he couldn't have … no, he was in deep shit because the fucking condom broke, and he didn't even know her name.

He ran a hand over his head and stared at the condom in the trash. At twenty-eight, he'd never lost control with a woman, and he'd never had a condom malfunction. Maybe he'd just been lucky to this point, but all bets were off now. He still didn't know how she'd gotten into the apartment, or why she'd crawled into his bed. What had seemed like a gift too good to pass up just moments ago, now felt more like a noose tightening around his neck.

Fuck!

Drake pulled on his jeans and his Army t-shirt, shoved his feet back into his boots, and rushed downstairs, in hopes his brother hadn't left yet. The bar was dark, and the door was locked. Dallas was nowhere to be seen and his truck was gone from the lot. Drake reached for his cell and realized he'd left it upstairs. He'd have no choice but to go back up and try to wake the sleeping beauty in his bed and hope for some coherent answers.

Soft snores greeted his ears as he neared his bedroom, and he had to admit she looked rather adorable sprawled across his bed. Her red hair fanned out around her, and he ached to crawl in beside her, just to hold her until morning light, when he'd have to face reality. Why couldn't anything in his life ever be simple? He'd been in the Army for ten years, had been in Afghanistan more days of the year than he'd been home. After tonight, he'd be the Army's perfect soldier for the next six months in the godforsaken desert. And then his time would finally be up, and he'd be able to get on with his life.

Hell, he wasn't even sure how to live outside of the Army. What was he going to do with his time? He technically owned the bar with his brother, but could he really hack civilian life? He'd have to find out soon enough.

He shot off a text to his brother, asking about the mysterious woman now hogging the bed, and then shut off the lamp. Nudging her over some, he slid into bed beside her and stared up at the ceiling. His phone dinged, and he picked it up, squinting at the screen in the dark.

Dallas: She's stranded and needed a place to stay. She's also completely sauced.

Great. Just fucking great. He'd not only taken advantage of a damsel in distress, but she'd been too drunk to know what the hell she was doing. Now he really felt like an ass. He'd never taken a woman against her will, and it sickened him that she might not have consented if she'd been thinking clearly. Drake wasn't sure if he wanted her to be awake before he left so they could talk, or if it was better to slip away and let his brother deal with the fallout. He'd never been one to take the coward's way out, but it was mighty damn tempting this time.

Chapter Two

Three months later

Shiloh's hand covered her mouth as she rushed through the bar to the bathroom down the back hall. She didn't even want to think about what might be on the sticky floor as she fell to her knees and lost her dinner. Whoever coined the term morning sickness should be taken out and shot. As far as Shiloh could tell, it was all damn day sickness. She didn't know how much longer she could keep the baby a secret. People were getting suspicious already, and she could only claim a stomach bug for so long.

Her throat burned as she threw up again, the scent making her gag some more. Shiloh flushed the toilet and got off the nasty floor. She turned on the sink and rinsed out her mouth before splashing cool water on her face. The bathroom door banged open, and Dallas stood silhouetted in the doorway, his imposing figure making her cringe. This was going to go one of two ways. He was going to find out and be supportive, or he was going to ask her to get the hell out his bar and never darken his doorstep again.

"Don't even try to tell me it's a bug," he said in a no-nonsense tone. "You've been throwing up consistently for over two weeks. Tell me which asshole is responsible, and I'll pound the shit out of him until he takes responsibility."

Resigned, she turned and met his gaze. There had only been one man she'd been with since coming to Gulch Springs, and her ex hadn't touched her for weeks prior to that. There was only one possible baby-daddy in this scenario, and Dallas was *not* going to be happy about it. She'd never told him the truth of what happened the night he'd given her shelter, and she doubted Drake had come clean either.

"I can wait all night," Dallas said. "We're not leaving this bathroom until you give me a name."

"Can't you just leave it alone?"

"Are you keeping the baby?' he asked.

It had never crossed her mind *not* to keep the baby. It was a part of her, and despite the circumstances around the poor bean's conception, she already loved the child with all her heart.

"I'm keeping it."

"Then the daddy needs to fork over some cash to help you out. Don't forget that I've seen where you live, Shiloh. That rusted heap isn't fit for you to live in, much less a baby. And what are you going to do about a job?"

Her stomach clenched. "You're firing me?"

"Hell no, but you can't bring a baby with you to the bar. Not to mention all the secondhand smoke. And what about childcare? There's nowhere around town that's open nights, especially the hours you work. If your kid sleeps at night, they're going to be awake all day. You can't leave them alone while you sleep. This job isn't the right fit for you anymore."

He made valid points, but she wasn't ready to think about it yet.

"A name, Shiloh."

She shook her head. "It's better if you don't know."

"Shiloh, I think of you as a sister, and I want to help, but I can't do that if you won't let me in. You don't talk to anyone but Rebecca and me, and you never go out on dates. I have no idea how you managed to get knocked up. You haven't had time for it."

She stared at the toes of her boots.

"Darlin', if you won't talk to me, will you at least talk to Rebecca? You know we think of you like family, but there's only so much I can do if you keep silent."

"She knows," Shiloh mumbled. It hadn't been on purpose, but during one of her crying spells, she'd spilled everything to Rebecca, whom she'd sworn to secrecy. In hindsight, it was wrong of her to put her friend in that position. She'd asked her to lie to Dallas.

The look in Dallas's eyes turned dark, and he spun on his boot heel and marched back out into the bar, probably heading straight for his doting fiancée. Shiloh scrambled after him. He faced his fiancée with his hands planted on his hips and stern look on his face. Rebecca blinked up at him, the picture of innocence.

"You knew she was pregnant and didn't say anything?" Dallas asked.

"It wasn't my story to tell." Rebecca shrugged. "If she wanted you to know, she'd have told you."

"Nice." He snorted. "You realize she's in no position to take care of herself right now, much less a baby. So, what's your bright idea?"

Rebecca looked at Shiloh, her eyes begging Shiloh to tell the truth, but it was a secret that could destroy her. She didn't want to lose the only friends she had in Gulch Springs. The locals were friendly enough and tipped decently, but no one exactly asked her to hang out on her days off. She'd been hit on more times than she could count, but that wasn't the same thing.

"He needs to know," Rebecca said.

Tears gathered in Shiloh's eyes. *Stupid pregnancy hormones.*

Dallas claimed the seat next to Rebecca and waited patiently. Shiloh didn't want to disappoint him. Dallas had been wonderful to her, so had Rebecca. If it weren't for the two of them, she'd have ended up on the streets after she'd been dumped in this very bar. Dallas had given her a job, and Rebecca had let her crash on her couch until she'd saved enough to rent the trailer she had now. Neither of them had been happy with her choice of residence, but she'd wanted to stand on her own two feet as soon as possible.

"He's not going to be mad at you," Rebecca assured her. "Just tell him. Please. It's killing me to keep it from him."

Dallas stared her down.

"I didn't tell you about the pregnancy because of who the father is," Shiloh said.

Rebecca gave her a nod of encouragement.

"It's … the father is…" Her hands twisted in front of her. This was harder than she'd thought. "It's Drake."

He blinked slowly and then looked at Rebecca before that blue gaze clashed with hers again. "Excuse me?"

"The night you let me stay at your place? I didn't know which room was yours and I ended up falling asleep in Drake's room. He came home and…" She shrugged. "I was drunk, but I promise it was consensual."

"Why the hell didn't you say something sooner?" Dallas asked. "I'd have notified him so he could come home and do the right thing."

Shiloh's brow furrowed. "This isn't 1950. There's no 'right thing' to do. The baby is mine, and I'm going to love him and raise him the best I can. I hope you'll be part of the baby's life since you're his uncle, but if you'd rather I made myself scarce, I'll understand."

Dallas rose and pulled her in for a tight hug. "You have my support. I don't agree with keeping the pregnancy a secret from Drake, but I won't force the issue. He'll find out sooner or later. You only have three months before he comes home."

"I don't want him rushing home because he fathered a baby with a woman he doesn't even know. For all I know, he doesn't even remember me or that night. What if he comes back and has no idea who I am?"

Dallas stepped back. "Whether he recognizes you or not, you need to tell him the truth. I don't know what the hell he'll say, or what he'll do, but I can promise he won't leave you to figure everything out on your own. Drake was raised right, and I have no doubt that he'll want to be part of the baby's life, even if that means he pays child support for the next eighteen years."

"I need this job, Dallas. I don't have the training to do much else. Who's going to hire a pregnant woman anyway? They'll know maternity leave is coming, and no one wants to deal with that."

"You have bigger things to worry about. You need to see a doctor, and you don't have insurance. I could put you on the bar's plan, but I don't know if they'll cover the pregnancy. Pre-existing condition, or some such nonsense."

"I'll give her a ride to the clinic tomorrow," Rebecca offered. "It's better than nothing."

"The clinic is fine for getting a pregnancy test done, just as confirmation, but that baby deserves a better doctor than that place can offer. She needs to see Dr. Thompson. His father delivered every baby in my family while he was practicing medicine, and his son seems to be a great doctor too."

Rebecca shook her head.

"What?' Dallas asked. "You have a better idea? She can't just coast along until Drake gets home."

"I'll be fine," Shiloh said. "I took three pregnancy tests, so I don't think I really need confirmation, and I already picked up some of those prenatal vitamins at the store. I have everything I need for right now."

"If he makes it home alive, he's going to have worry about *me* killing him," Dallas said with a shake of his head. "How could he have been so stupid as to not use protection?"

"You don't know what happened," Rebecca pointed out. "Maybe he did, and it just didn't work. Condoms aren't foolproof."

"Obviously." Dallas hugged Shiloh again. "You let me know if you need anything, okay? And I mean that. You have trouble paying a bill or buying food, you come tell me. That's my niece or nephew incubating in there, and I want to take care of y'all until my idiot brother gets home to do the job."

"I've been doing just fine on my own," Shiloh said. "I know you don't approve of where I live, but there's plenty of room for both the baby and me. I haven't used the second bedroom for anything, so I can make it a nursery."

"And what money are you going to use to buy a crib and diapers and crap?" Dallas looked like he was counting to ten before he started back up. "I'm going to find you a better job, with better pay, and you're going to promise me that you'll move to a safer place. That trailer park is a known beacon for drug addicts and prostitution. I won't have that baby growing up there. You both deserve better."

"You could always let her move into your room in the apartment," Rebecca said. "It's not like you really use it. No reason you can't bring your things to my place, since you're there every night anyway. We're getting married in less than a year. Sooner or later, your stuff is going to comingle with mine."

"I'm not pushing anyone out of their room," Shiloh said. "Besides, then I'd have to share the apartment with Drake, and that would be a disaster."

"Actually, I think it's fucking brilliant," Dallas said. "I'll have my stuff out by tomorrow night. If you need help packing, just say the word."

Shiloh shook her head.

"This isn't up for debate, Shiloh," Dallas said. "You're family, and I always take care of my family. And stop shaking your head at me. I wasn't asking you to move. I'm telling you to move."

A fire lit in her belly, or maybe it was indigestion. It was hard to tell these days.

"I paid for my place out of my own pocket, and I intend to keep paying my way. See, this is why I didn't say anything. I knew you'd go all caveman on me, or worse, force Drake to walk me down the aisle over a mistake that was made on a night when I was too drunk to know better. I'm not punishing him or anyone else for what happened. I'm staying in my trailer until I can afford something better *on my own*, and that's final."

Dallas glowered, but Rebecca rubbed his back.

"If she wants to be independent, let her," Rebecca said. "It's not like you don't know where she lives. You can check on her anytime you want."

"Fine. I don't like it, but I'm obviously not going to win." Dallas raked a hand through his hair. "You can't keep working here though. The secondhand smoke isn't good for the baby, and if I make this a no-smoking zone, then I'll lose business to the bar on the other side of town."

"So, this is my last night?" Shiloh asked.

"No, this was your last minute. Go get your stuff and head home."

Shiloh felt a little like a kicked puppy as she stamped her timecard for the last time and put it in the slot with her name. She gathered her belongings from the locker in the break room and went out to her piece-of-crap car with as much dignity as she could muster. The door creaked and groaned as she opened it. After tossing her things onto the passenger seat, she slid behind the wheel and closed her door. Or attempted to. It had taken four times before it stopped bouncing back open, and then she locked it, in hopes it would remain shut while she was driving.

Her trailer was in the Shady Pines Trailer Park in one of the worst parts of town. Not that Gulch Springs had a high crime rate. She liked living in the small town, which had surprised her. When Shiloh had been abandoned, she'd thought she'd work enough hours to scrape together some cash and get the heck out of here. Instead, she'd decided to rent a place and put down roots. She didn't regret her decision, but she might when Drake came back home.

The trailer park was dimly lit as she pulled down the drive and past the front office. She wound her way around toward the back where her rusted heap resided. The streetlight near her place had been out for a few weeks, and it was eerily dark when she pulled onto the parking pad next to her home. Her porch light didn't work, even when there was a new bulb in it. Dallas thought it had a short, but the office didn't seem too intent on fixing it, and she couldn't afford an electrician.

Using the light on her iPhone, she managed to open the door and carry her things inside. Shiloh flicked on the living room lamp and dropped everything beside the couch. She locked the door—knob, bolt, and chain—before going into the bathroom to start the shower. It was going to get cramped in the tiny space once she started to show, but at least the water was hot. All right, so it was warm. Better than ice cold, so she wasn't going to complain.

Shiloh ditched her clothes and stepped under the

spray, washing the smoke off her skin and out of her hair. She always showered when she came home from the bar so she wouldn't make her sheets stinky. She only had the one pair, and there wasn't a washing machine or dryer in her home. If she wanted clean clothes and bedding, she had to use the laundromat, or head over to Rebecca's if she was low on cash, which she'd done a few times already. Her friend had assured her that she wasn't taking advantage, even if it didn't feel like that was the case.

Squeaky clean, she shut off the water and dried off with one of her three-dollar towels. In the bedroom, she pulled on a pair of sleep shorts and a tank, and then pulled her hair into a messy bun. The problem with working nights was that she was always keyed up when she got home. Tonight was no different, except she didn't have a job to return to tomorrow. Shiloh spent the next hour watching a really horrible movie and munching on some popcorn from the dollar store. When she was finally tired enough to sleep, she fell into bed and prayed that things would look better tomorrow. Who the hell was going to hire her?

****

Drake used the webcam on his laptop to Skype with his brother. He knew it was early morning for Dallas, but the bar had been closed at least an hour, which meant his brother's responsibilities were over for the night. He looked haggard, and Drake worried about him. Dallas was always full of life and ready to take on any challenge, but for the first time since their parents died, he seemed a little worn around the edges.

"Not getting enough sleep?" Drake asked.

"Just dealing with something. A friend is going through a hard time right now, and I'm not sure how to help her."

Drake smiled. "You have to stop taking in these

damsels. You're going to get a rep as a white knight, and then they'll all be flocking to your bar wanting a handout."

"If only money solved everything." Dallas shook his head. "Forget about me, how are you holding up over there?"

Drake shrugged. "About as well as can be expected. I only have three months until I get to come home, and I am counting the days!"

"It will be really great to have you home. For good this time, right?"

"Yeah, it's for good. My soldiering days are over, or close to it. I'm ready to get a regular job, work my way through all the eligible ladies, and just kick back with some beers. Hell, I may even stop for some fun on the way home from the airport. No sense coming home empty handed."

Dallas looked troubled by his comment.

"You're not going to get all brotherly on me and tell me that I'm fucking up my life, are you? Because sleeping my way through the surrounding towns isn't really a bad way to go. It's been three fucking months since I got laid and I have the worst case of blue balls."

"We need to talk when you get back. Might be best if you put those plans on hold for a night or two."

"Everything okay with the bar? With Rebecca?"

"My life is just fine, brother. Yours…" Dallas shook his head. "It can wait until you're back home. Just come back in one piece, will ya?"

"You bet." Drake smiled despite the uneasy feeling in his gut. Something was going on at home, and for whatever reason, his brother didn't want to discuss it. He couldn't think of anything that would cause his brother to lose sleep other than the bar or his fiancée, and since Dallas said it wasn't either one of those things…

"Take care of yourself," Dallas said. "You have a lot to live for."

He was half-owner of the bar and shared a place with his brother. What exactly did he have to live for? Dallas wasn't making any damn sense.

"I'll see you soon," Drake said. "I'll try to Skype again in a week or two, just to check in."

"See that you do. Miss you."

Drake's throat tightened. "Miss you too."

They signed off, and Drake shoved the laptop away. Whatever was going on with Dallas, he couldn't focus on it right now. He was in the middle of a war, and while he didn't know if they would ever win, he did intend to go home in a few months, and not in a body bag. If he didn't keep his head in the game, someone was going to blow it off.

Chapter Three

Shiloh hiked her purse over her shoulder and tugged on her denim skirt and brushed off her off-the-shoulder blouse. It wasn't fancy, but it was the nicest thing she had. So far, she'd been turned down for every job she'd applied for. It had been two weeks since Dallas let her go. The library said she wasn't qualified, even though their ad said no experience necessary. The Stop 'N Go didn't feel comfortable with an expectant mother handling the night shift, in case of a robbery. She'd even stopped by the newspaper office to see about delivering papers, but they'd deemed her car a hazard and unfit for the job. There weren't too many options for employment around Gulch Springs, but it seemed that every door was slamming in her face.

She stared at the trailer on the construction company's latest job site. When she'd called the main number, she'd been assured the owner would be here and could see her at eleven. It was now three minutes to eleven, and she wiped her hands on her skirt. With a hesitant knock on the door, she waited for someone to answer.

A burly guy in a hard hat, stained t-shirt, and threadbare jeans opened the door. If he was the owner, she wasn't sure she wanted the job. He eyed her from head to toe, paying a little too much attention to the girls, who had grown considerably during the pregnancy. She was about two seconds from popping out of her top, but she couldn't exactly afford a new wardrobe right now, so what she owned would have to suffice.

"Can I help you, sweet thing?" he asked before taking a bite of the cheeseburger in his hand.

Shiloh prayed she wouldn't throw up on his shoes as she watched him chew with his mouth open. Her stomach rolled, and she pressed a hand against it, praying that she could keep it together just long enough to either get the job or a send-off.

"I'm here to see Mr. Latimer."

He gestured toward the inside of the trailer. "He's in the office in the back. Go on through."

She smiled and tried to squeeze past without touching him, and then wandered down the short hall to the office in the back. A man in his late thirties or early forties sat behind a metal desk, strewn with papers and discarded cups of coffee. His hair was turning silver along his sideburns, and he looked a little harried.

"Mr. Latimer?" She ventured a little further inside. "I called earlier about the ad in the paper, for a general office clerk."

He looked up, skimmed her head to toe, and then his gaze held steady on hers. "You ever worked for a construction company before?"

She shook her head. "I've mostly waited tables. Diners. Bars. But I'm really good with people, and I know if given a chance that I could do this job. I learn things quickly."

"This job is fast paced and stressful. You don't look like you could handle either of those things. What makes you want this job so badly?"

"The truth?" She tugged on her purse strap. "I'm pregnant, and I've been without a job for two weeks. Rent is due soon, and my pantry is about empty. I need a job in the worst way, and I'll do whatever you ask."

"When can you start?"

"Is today too soon?" She smiled.

"You're not even going to ask about pay or benefits?"

"Any pay is better than none, and I didn't have benefits at my last job. I will need maternity leave in about six months, though. Is that going to be a problem?"

He shook his head. "I could hire a temp while you're out. Why don't you fill out an application? While you wait up front, I'll call and check your references, and then we'll see where we stand."

"I don't really have any references except for Dallas Edwards and Rebecca Taft."

Mr. Latimer sat back in his chair. "I know Dallas rather well. If he vouches for you, then you're hired."

"Thank you."

He handed her an application and a pen. Shiloh went to the desk out front and sat down to complete the form. She hoped her tendency to leave jobs after a few months wouldn't hurt her. If Dallas hadn't fired her, she'd have stayed at the bar for as long as possible. Deep down, she knew he was right. The bar wasn't a good fit for her anymore. She only hoped being around all that smoke for the last three months hadn't harmed her child. The moment she'd realized she was pregnant, she'd stopped drinking.

When she finished filling out the blanks, she picked up the application and carried it back to Mr. Latimer. He accepted it with a smile and told her to wait out front while he looked things over. Shiloh fought the urge to bite her nails as she waited, hoping that he'd give her the job. He hadn't mentioned pay, and she didn't much care what it was, as long as she could afford rent, utilities, and food. Anything else was just extra.

"Miss Anderson?" Mr. Latimer appeared by her side. How she hadn't heard him, she'd never know. "Why don't you come back to my office and we'll discuss a few things."

She nodded and followed him down the hall, claiming the chair across from his.

"Dallas told me how the two of you met and that

you've done a wonderful job at his bar. He also explained that he had to fire you because of your condition, for your own good. From what I've heard, and what I've seen on the application, I'm willing to give you a chance. Ninety days' probation, during which time I can fire you without penalty if things don't work out. I'll start you at nine dollars an hour, which I know is a little low, but if you make it past the ninety days, I'll increase it to ten."

"Thank you."

"The job is forty hours a week, seven to four. You get an hour for lunch. There are health benefits, as well as holiday pay. Once your probation is over, I'll give you five days of sick time and five days of vacation. Just make sure you ask for the vacation at least a few weeks in advance so I can plan accordingly."

"You're really giving me the job?" she asked.

He smiled. "Yes, I am. You can start tomorrow. The desk out front where you were sitting will be yours. When this job is finished, the trailer will move to another job site, and you'll report there."

Shiloh bolted out of her seat, a wide smile on her face. "You won't regret this, Mr. Latimer. I promise to work hard."

"I'll see you at seven tomorrow."

She paused. "About the dress code?"

"Jeans are fine. Try not to wear anything too revealing. Some of these guys can be complete horn dogs. Even your pregnancy won't keep them from hitting on you. If anything, it might make it worse. There's just something about a pregnant woman that makes a man think impure thoughts."

Shiloh shook her head. "I'm sure I've handled worse at the bar."

"If you have too much trouble, you just let me

know."

"Thank you, Mr. Latimer."

He smiled. "Shiloh, I'm not that old. Mr. Latimer is my dad. Just call me Charlie."

"Thank you, Charlie."

He winked. "I'll see you bright and early. We'll start out slow until you get the hang of things. Enjoy your last day of freedom. Oh, paydays are every Friday, but there's a week lag. So, whatever hours you work this week will be paid next Friday."

"It will be nice to have some money coming in again."

"If you get in a tight spot before your first check, you let me know. A pregnant lady shouldn't do without."

She thanked him again and went back out to her car. It was a little embarrassing when it took six tries before the door shut and then another three minutes before the engine turned over. The car backfired, and a black plume of smoke came from the muffler as she pulled out of the space and headed back toward her trailer. Maybe after she worked on getting a better rental, she could focus on getting a better car. It wasn't safe to drive her pregnant self around in the car, much less a newborn.

At her trailer, she raided the cabinets until she found a can of SpaghettiOs. She pulled a plastic bowl from the cabinet next to the sink, dumped the pasta into the dish, and then microwaved it for two minutes. It wasn't the lunch of champions, but it would stop her stomach from growling. Although, she was hungry an awful lot lately. She knew it wouldn't be long before she was starving again, and there was hardly anything left to eat.

A knock sounded at the door, and she abandoned her food to answer it. Rebecca stood on her stoop, laden with plastic grocery sacks. Shiloh crossed her arms and stared her friend down. She'd told Rebecca several times that she would be fine and didn't need any help, and now that she had a job, things were looking up. It was only a week and a half until she was paid, even if it wouldn't be a full week of pay.

"What are those?" Shiloh asked with a pointed look at the sacks.

"Just a little something from Dallas and me, and before you send me away, think about the baby. I know you're not eating enough. Despite the fact you're several months pregnant, I think you're actually losing weight."

"I'm fine, Rebecca."

"Are you going to let me in?"

Shiloh sighed and took a step back. Rebecca went straight to the kitchen and set the sacks on the counter. Shiloh reached into a bag and pulled out a bunch of bananas and a bag of grapes. She also found some apples and oranges in the sack. It had been a while since she'd been able to afford this much fruit. The cheap stuff at the store was all the crap that was bad for her, while the yummy fruits and veggies would break the bank.

When they finished putting things away, she had a bunch of yogurt, some applesauce, milk, orange juice, and her freezer was filled with meat. Rebecca put the last of the canned goods away and stuffed the empty sacks under the sink. She leaned against the counter and studied Shiloh.

"I know you're probably going to say no, but I thought I could take you to my favorite salon. We could get your hair and nails done before your job starts tomorrow. Have a girls' day." Rebecca smiled. "My treat. I want to do something nice for you."

"Rebecca, y'all spent enough on food. I'm sure there's about two hundred dollars of crap in my cabinets and fridge now. While I appreciate the fact Dallas and you want to look after me, I need to stand on my own two feet." She leaned against the wall and slid down until her knees pressed against her chest. "How can I take care of a baby if I can't even feed myself? I'm only going to bring home around $300 a week."

Rebecca kneeled in front of her. "Hey. You're doing great, Shiloh. Really. If I were pregnant and alone, I'd be freaking the fuck out. You could have taken the easy way out and had Dallas talk to Drake, tell him what's going on, but you want to go it alone. I respect that, but I think you should hold Drake accountable. This child isn't just yours. It's part of Drake too, and even if he doesn't want to be there every day for the two of you, you should at least accept some financial support from him. It's the least he can do."

Shiloh didn't want to admit that her friend might be right. How was she supposed to tell some stranger that she was pregnant with his child? They hadn't even exchanged names that night. She was just some nameless woman who had crashed in his bed, and she'd hoped it would remain that way. There was a chance he'd recognize her when he came home, but what if he didn't? How weird would it be to confront him about the baby if he didn't even remember being with her?

"You have three months to figure it out," Rebecca said. "But the moment Drake sees you, he's going to put two and two together. He's not stupid, Shiloh. Well, not usually. What he did that night definitely counts as stupid, though. I still can't believe he slept with you, didn't get your name, and then snuck out while you were sleeping. He was definitely a douche that day."

Shiloh cracked a smile. "I didn't exactly introduce myself or ask for his name, although I was pretty sure he was the brother Dallas had mentioned. I knew when I chose that room there was a fifty/fifty chance that I would end up in the wrong bed, but I was too drunk to care."

"I know you have your pride, but think about the baby. Drake may not be rolling in money, but he's made enough in the Army that he can take care of his child. Make him do his part."

"I'll think about it."

Rebecca nodded. "Now, how about that salon day?"

Shiloh shook her head. "You aren't going to give up, are you?"

"Nope."

"All right. I'll go."

Rebecca smiled widely and helped her to her feet. They rode together to Rosa's Hair & Nails. The sign wasn't fancy, and neither was the name, but everything in the salon was top notch. The vivacious Hispanic woman who owned the place whirled through the shop like a dervish, or maybe a social butterfly. She flitted from one place to another, checking on everyone. The girl assigned to Shiloh seemed young, but she had plenty of confidence as she studied Shiloh's mop of hair.

"I don't want it short," Shiloh said.

The girl lifted the heavy mass. "What if we took about four or five inches off? It would still hit the middle of your back. We could even add some highlights. Nothing too dramatic, unless you'd like some color?"

"My hair is already red. Are highlights really necessary?"

"Highlights would just brighten the color a little."

"I think you should wait," Rebecca said. "I don't know if you should color your hair while you're pregnant."

The girl standing behind her gave her a horrified

look in the mirror. "You're not even supposed to be in a salon around all these chemicals if you're pregnant. We have a special room in the back for expecting mothers, away from all the fumes. I can cut your hair back there."

"She was getting a mani/pedi too," Rebecca said.

"We can do that back there too," the girl said. "It's not a problem."

"Go on," Rebecca said. "You'll enjoy a little pampering. I'll be waiting when you're finished."

Shiloh followed the stylist into the back room and sat in the chair in front of the sink. She let the girl wash her hair before moving to the chair where it would get cut. Shiloh closed her eyes as she listened to the *snick* of the scissors and prayed the girl knew what she was doing. It was the first time in years she'd had her hair cut, and she was more than a little nervous. There wasn't a clock in the room, but it felt like hours had passed before she was handed a mirror and the chair was spun.

There was a hint of curl to her hair now that it was shorter and lighter. The red tresses were at the middle of her back, which would be more manageable when the baby arrived. Even the front looked good with some longer layers that framed her face. Overall, she was very pleased and wished she'd thought to get her hair cut a lot sooner.

"It looks great," Shiloh said.

The girl beamed. The next hour was spent on her mani/pedi, and when she was finished, Shiloh felt like a new woman. If only she could afford some new clothes too, but that would have to wait. Even though her kitchen was now well-stocked, she still wouldn't get a full paycheck for about two weeks. The good news was the rent was paid until the first. She'd have to tackle one problem at a time and get on some sort of schedule to make sure everything was paid, now that she didn't have tip money coming in every night. Weekly checks would take some adjustment, but it was worth it to have a nice desk job during the daytime. Things were looking up.

Rebecca was waiting for her when she stepped back out front.

"Wow. You look fantastic!" Rebecca smiled. "Drake won't know what hit him when he comes home. You were gorgeous before, but now you're absolutely stunning."

Shiloh snorted. "By the time he comes home, I'll be the size of a whale."

"You're barely showing. I bet you're going to have one of those pregnant figures that men just salivate over. With my luck, I'll be the size of a house, all swollen and puffy, and waddle everywhere I go."

"Are you…"

Rebecca shook her head. "No, but we've talked about it. Dallas wants to wait until after the wedding, and I can respect that. I'm not getting any younger though. I'll be thirty-two this year, and while I have plenty of friends who haven't had kids yet, I've heard the closer you get to forty the harder the pregnancy can be."

"I'm twenty-four, and trust me, it's no picnic. Morning sickness is a myth. I have all day sickness."

"I wish you'd see the doctor. You know Dallas would cover the cost of the visit."

Shiloh shook her head. She hadn't told anyone, but she'd gone to the free clinic for a check-up the other day. The doctor had taken her to task for her weight gain, or lack thereof, and written her a prescription for prenatal vitamins. Apparently, the ones over the counter weren't good enough, but she hadn't had the money to get it filled yet. She knew Dallas would pay for it if she told him, but she didn't want to feel like a charity case.

"What time do you have to be at work

tomorrow?" Rebecca asked.

"Seven."

"Wow, you're going to need an early bedtime if you're going to get any rest. Do you have time to stop for an early dinner before I take you back home? We could just pop in the diner down the street. I'm sure there's stuff you need to go prep for tomorrow."

Her stomach rumbled, but she wasn't about to let Rebecca buy her dinner after everything else she'd done for her today.

"I think I'd rather go home," she said. "Besides, you brought all that great food to me today. I might as well make something with it."

"We didn't put any meat in the fridge though. It's all frozen."

"I'll figure something out. Really, Rebecca. You've done too much for me already. I'll probably eat something light and get some sleep. I'm pretty worn out. The last two weeks have been stressful while I hunted for a job."

Rebecca nodded and drove them back to Shiloh's trailer. Shiloh waved to her as she opened the front door and slipped inside. The air from her window unit cooled her heated skin. She might be roasting now, but by winter she'd be freezing her ass off if she didn't move. The place hadn't come with working heat and air. She'd bought the window unit with her own money a few weeks after moving in. It had been a great investment, but it was definitely going with her when she moved. If she moved. At this rate, she had no idea how she was going to save for another place before her ninety days were up. If her calculations were right, she'd make around twelve hundred a month at her new job. That wasn't going to go far with a baby in the house. She didn't want to be one of those parents who had to work two jobs and never saw their kid. Maybe Rebecca was right, and she should accept a little help from Drake, assuming he didn't turn tail and run for the hills the moment he found out.

Only one way to find out. Waiting was no longer an option, not if she wanted to provide a safe home for her child.

Shiloh shot off a text to Dallas, asking for Drake's contact information. A moment later, her phone pinged with an email address. Thankfully, she had her email on her phone. A laptop had been a luxury she couldn't afford, at least not right now.

TO: SgtDrakeEdwards@army.us
FROM: TrblMkr1992@gmail.com
RE: The night you left

Sgt. Edwards,
You don't know me. Well, you actually know me rather well, but we didn't exactly exchange names the night before you shipped out. I'm the woman you found in your bed. I hate to do this through email, but I don't know how else to reach you. My name is Shiloh Anderson, and I worked for your brother at the bar for the last three months. The night you found me I'd been abandoned in town by someone I trusted. Dallas has been great, but I can't ask him to lie to you, even by omission.
I guess I should just come right out and say it.
I'm pregnant. And you're the father.
I realize you're overseas and you're fighting in a war. I'm not expecting you to hop the next plane home and come rescue me. I have a job at Latimer Construction and my own place, even if it's not much. It didn't seem fair to wait until you returned home to tell you about the baby. I'll be six months along by then.

You can have as little, or as much, to do with the baby as you want. I'm not giving it up. I went to the clinic the other day, and they estimate my due date for March 7th.

I hope you don't find this news too upsetting. Please stay safe.

Shiloh

As an afterthought, she snapped a picture of herself and attached it, just in case he was a little fuzzy on what happened that night. Maybe seeing her face would trigger something for him. Before she chickened out, she hit send, and then chewed on her bottom lip as she wondered if she'd done the right thing. She hoped like hell this didn't come back to bite her in the ass.

****

Drake felt ready to drop by the time he made it back to his bunk. The first thing he was going to do was wash all the damn sand off his body. Then he was going to get a bite to eat before checking to see if he had any messages from his brother. He gathered a change of clothes and his shower gel that doubled as shampoo and headed for the showers. He really loved the care packages Dallas and Rebecca sent.

Lingering in the shower wasn't a luxury he was afforded, not until he returned home.

By the time he was clean, dressed, and fed, his body was begging for some sleep. Before he crashed for a few hours, he pulled up his email and frowned when he saw an address he didn't recognize. Clicking on it, he read the email and felt his breath freeze in his lungs as his heart thumped out of control.

Oh, he remembered his last night at home all right and hadn't been able to get the passionate woman out of his head. He hadn't realized the Shiloh his brother had mentioned was the same woman, and he sure as hell hadn't known she was pregnant—with *his* kid. What the fuck? Why hadn't Dallas said something?

Drake stared at the screen, frozen. Was he supposed to email her back? What the hell should he say? He was halfway around the world and couldn't exactly pop home for a visit. His fingers dug into his scalp as his heart raced out of control. He'd never really thought about having kids before, but if he'd gotten Shiloh pregnant, it was a little late now.

Panic gave way to anger. Just because she claimed the kid was his didn't mean it was true. The kind of woman who spread her legs for some random stranger probably got around. Despite the fact she had his brother fooled, Drake wasn't going to just take her at her word. He was going to need something more than a home pregnancy test to tell him he was a daddy. If she expected any sort of compensation from him, she'd better have a damn paternity test done. He might not be rich, but he was comfortable enough that some barfly probably thought he would be a good payday.

His teeth ground together as he emailed her back.

TO: TrblMkr1992@gmail.com
FROM: SgtDrakeEdwards@army.us
RE: RE: The night you left
Miss Anderson,
You'll have to pardon me if I don't accept your word that you're carrying my kid. A woman who sleeps with a random stranger has probably made the rounds. If you're expecting some sort of compensation from me, I'm going to have to demand a paternity test. This isn't something I can deal with right now.
If I'm the father, I'll do right by you and provide for my son or daughter. I left a toothbrush at the apartment that

Dallas can use for my DNA. Unless you're lying, you shouldn't have any reason to avoid having the test done. And if you are lying, I'd appreciate it if you'd leave my family the hell alone. They don't need this kind of shit dropped at their door.
Sgt. Edwards

He hit send before he could change his mind. The voice in his head was kicking his ass for possibly upsetting a pregnant woman, but he needed to know if she was a gold digger out for an easy ride. She couldn't be making that much and had to be looking for an easy way out. After that email, he'd either be free of her, or he'd be making plans to buy baby furniture when got home. The thought nauseated him a little. Babies scared the crap out of him.

Chapter Four

Shiloh's hands clenched into fists, and her teeth nearly ground to dust as she read the email from Drake Edwards. How that vile man could possibly be related to Dallas, she'd never understand. They couldn't possibly be more different. When she'd named Drake as the father of her baby, Dallas hadn't hesitated to take her word for it and give her his support. Her baby-daddy, however, was an asshole who needed his ass kicked. If he thought she'd accept a penny of his money, he'd better think again. For all she cared, he could roast in hell after that email.

A paternity test, indeed.

She finished dressing for work before shooting off a text to Dallas.

Shiloh: Your brother is an asshole.

Dallas: I won't argue. I heard about the email.

Shiloh: I'm never speaking to him again.

She jammed her phone into her purse, grabbed her keys, and stormed out the door, letting it slam shut behind her. After five attempts to crank her car engine, she was finally on her way to work, a thick cloud of smoke trailing after her. She might have a POS car, and her trailer might be just as shitty, but at least she was standing on her own two feet. Not once did she ask Drake Edwards for a handout, and she sure as fuck wouldn't now. This baby was her responsibility. She'd raise it on her own and to hell with Drake Edwards.

By the time Shiloh reached the construction site, she no longer had a death grip on the steering wheel, and her temper had cooled a little. She slammed her car door and cursed as it bounced back open. Her ballet flats were the only thing keeping her from kicking the shit out of her car.

Mr. Latimer leaned against a tree and shook his head. "I think you need a new car."

"Cars take money," she said as she approached him. "I hope I'm not late. It's been a rough morning."

"I'm surprised you made it at all, driving that death trap. You know, part of your job will be running some errands for me, or rather, for the office. How can I in good conscience send you around town in that thing?" he asked.

"It gets me where I need to go."

He eyed her car again before motioning for her to follow him into the trailer they called an office. She was surprised to see a laptop, a stapler, and a cup of pens on the desk she as to call her own. It had been completely bare when she'd last seen it. Her computer skills weren't all that great, but hopefully, she could manage any tasks he gave her. The laptop was shiny and obviously brand new.

"I set up the laptop for you this morning. Your login information is on a sticky note on the screen. There are legal pads in your desk drawer, and the supplies are stored in the hall closet if you need anything else. For the morning, why don't you just familiarize yourself with your new computer and answer any incoming calls? I'll have some other stuff for you to do after lunch."

She nibbled her lower lip. "You don't have to go easy on me."

"You're pregnant, Shiloh. This business can be fast paced, and I don't want to stress you out on your first day. We can ease into things until you get up to speed. Are there any upcoming doctor appointments I need to know about?"

"No. I mean, I went to the free clinic for an official pregnancy test, and they gave me a prescription for prenatal vitamins, but I don't have a regular doctor

I'm seeing."

He frowned. "That can't be good for the baby."

Shiloh folded her arms over her chest. "No offense, Mr. Latimer…"

"Charlie," he interrupted her. "We agreed you'd call me Charlie."

"Charlie." She sighed. "I appreciate the concern, but I'm healthy, and the baby is fine. You didn't mention anything about insurance, so I'm assuming there isn't any. If I think something is wrong, I'll go back to the free clinic."

"I'm sorry, Shiloh. I wasn't even thinking about insurance. There's a ninety-day waiting period usually, but given your condition, I think we'd better waive that."

She shook her head. "You're going to treat me the same as your other employees. If I need to see a doctor before the ninety days are up, I'll go to the clinic. Now, I think it's best if I get to work. And if there are errands that need to be run, I'm more than capable of going. My car may not be the prettiest thing in the parking lot, but like I said, it gets me where I need to go."

He muttered something under his breath as he went down the hall to his office.

Shiloh blew out a breath before storing her purse in an empty drawer of her new desk and taking a seat. Having a disagreement with her new boss hadn't been on the list of things to do this morning, but she hoped he understood that she wasn't a charity case. She'd never been afraid of hard work, and she wasn't going to start accepting handouts now. Her pregnancy complicated things a bit, but she was more than capable of taking care of herself and her child.

Although, the thought of all the baby things she would need terrified her. She'd done a little online shopping, or rather, online browsing, and it was crazy how expensive a bed and changing table were. And diapers! She was going to go broke just keeping the kid in diapers. From the little research she'd done online, she knew a lot of expectant moms had baby showers to get a lot of what they needed, but Shiloh was still relatively new to town, and her only friends were Dallas and Rebecca. It wasn't likely anyone else would show up if she had one.

The morning dragged by as she answered the few calls that came through, and she played with her new laptop. She probably wasn't supposed to use it for personal things, but she checked her email just to see if Sergeant Asshole had sent anything else. The only message in her inbox was from Rebecca with a flyer attached for a local church who helped expectant mothers. Shiloh had never been the religious type and figured it wasn't likely they'd help a sinner like her. The last time she'd set foot in a church had been for a cousin's funeral ten years ago.

Shiloh deleted the email before logging out. Her stomach rumbled, and she saw it was close to lunchtime. She hadn't discussed her lunch break with Charlie, and her dumb ass hadn't thought to pack one. All that food at home and she'd been so rattled this morning she hadn't even thought to grab a sandwich. She had an hour for lunch, so she could hurry home and get a bite to eat.

She stood and stretched before going down the hall and tapping on Charlie's open door.

"I hate to interrupt, but is it okay if I go to lunch?" she asked.

"Of course. I'm sorry, Shiloh. I should have told you that you can take lunch whenever you like. There are instructions in the desk for turning the voicemail on while you're gone, and instructions on how to check it when you get back. You never have to ask permission to go to lunch."

"I'm just going to run home and get something, but I'll be back before my hour is up."

He tipped his head. "Would you rather eat out? I wouldn't mind some company, and I was about to head over to the Blue Plate Diner. Lunch is on me. Consider it a Welcome to Latimer Construction-type of lunch."

"Oh, no. You've already done enough for me."

He waved away her concern. "I'd like a chance to get to know my new employee a little better. What do you say?"

She reluctantly agreed.

They took Charlie's truck to the diner and grabbed a seat by the window. Shiloh's stomach rumbled as she looked at the menu and her cheeks flushed. Charlie encouraged her to order whatever she wanted, even dessert. She felt a little awkward letting him pay for her meal, but she definitely couldn't afford to eat out until her first paycheck. And even then, she'd need it for rent.

"So, what brought you to our sleepy little town?" Charlie asked.

"My ex-boyfriend convinced me to move across country with him, and we made a pit stop along the way. He said he was going out to the truck for a moment, and the next thing I knew, I'd been stranded at the bar. Dallas gave me a place to sleep that first night and Rebecca let me crash on her couch until I could save enough for my own place."

"I saw on your application you're living at the trailer park across town." He toyed with the salt shaker. "I'm sure I don't have to tell you that isn't a safe place for a single woman, much less an expectant mother."

"It's what I can afford for now. Besides, it keeps

me dry in the rain, which is more than I can say for some of the places I've lived in before." She smiled. "I appreciate your concern, but I promise I'm fine."

"I'm not trying to pry. I'm going to tell you a story that you're bound to hear sooner or later anyway. When I was in college, my younger sister, a high school senior at the time, got pregnant. Her boyfriend refused to take responsibility, and my dad threw her out of the house. Shelly went down a spiral that no one could save her from, and I watched as she slowly destroyed herself and her child. I just don't want to see the same thing happen to you. Not once have you mentioned the father, so I'm assuming he's not in the picture."

She shook her head.

"Shelly is gone, and so is my nephew. I kept the things I found in the trailer where she was living. Not the same place where you live now, but a little further down the road. I'd like you to consider accepting the baby bed for your child. It's nothing fancy, and you'll need a mattress and bedding, but I think she would have wanted you to have it. It's just collecting dust in my attic right now."

"Charlie, I appreciate the offer, but I couldn't take something that means so much to you."

"Just think about it. I'd rather you get some use out of it than have it rot away up there. My wife can't have kids, so my family is never going to use it."

Shiloh nodded and hoped he wouldn't bring it up again. It was one thing to accept a job from him, but she didn't want to accept anything else. Even though he was obviously married, she wasn't taking a chance that he might think she owed him in some way. It wouldn't be the first time someone had wanted sexual favors for helping her out, and she doubted it would be the last.

The rest of lunch went smoothly, and when she

got back to the office, he handed her a stack of papers and showed her how to create files for the new job bids, and where to file the papers for the current job. The afternoon flew by and before long it was time to head home for the night. She poked her head into his office to let him know she was going, and then she crossed her fingers that her stupid car would start.

By the time she got home, her back ached and her feet were screaming from the uncomfortable cheap shoes. She'd gotten them at a thrift store, but even new they probably hadn't cost more than ten dollars. The soles were in good shape, but there was absolutely no padding inside of them, and they'd pinched her toes. At least she got to sit for most of her job. Maybe she could kick off her shoes under her desk tomorrow, and no one would notice.

Shiloh locked the door and went to her room to strip down. She filled the tub with warm water—since it was that or ice cold water—and added some bubbles. When it was full, she shut off the taps and sank into the lilac-scented warmth. The water only lapped at her ribs and almost her entire upper body was exposed, but she couldn't be picky. Shiloh relaxed in the tub until her fingers and toes started to prune. She slid down until her hair was submerged in the water and she shampooed it before getting out.

She'd thawed a package of chicken to eat over the next few days and cooked the three breasts with a package of Lipton rice. After she had fixed her plate, she stored the leftovers in the fridge to have for dinner over the next two nights. Or maybe she'd carry some of it to work tomorrow for lunch. She'd seen a microwave and fridge in the breakroom. Even though Charlie hadn't said she could use them, she assumed it would be all right.

When she was finished, she cleaned up and

grabbed a worn paperback to read until bedtime. She refused to check her email again and wondered if she'd made a big mistake telling Drake about the baby. Dallas had seemed so sure that his brother would want to know, but his response had been so angry and accusatory. He'd treated her like trash and basically called her a whore. Was that really the kind of man she wanted around her child?

He may have donated the DNA to make her baby, but she'd be damned if she'd let him anywhere near her child.

****

Drake read his brother's email and wondered if he'd made a mistake. Dallas seemed certain that Shiloh was telling the truth, and she even had Rebecca's support. But his brother had a soft spot for a damsel in distress, so Drake wasn't certain he could trust his brother on this one. Then again, if the woman really was the mother of his child, he'd treated her horribly. Dallas didn't seem to think she'd take the paternity test, not because she was lying but because she was hurt Drake had even asked for one.

He'd never had a pregnancy scare before and wasn't sure how to handle it, especially from so far away. There wasn't much he could do in the middle of the desert. Even if he believed her, it wasn't like he could marry her so she'd have access to his benefits. That would require him to be stateside, and that wasn't happening anytime soon. Besides, just because she was carrying his kid didn't mean he had to do something crazy like run off to Vegas with the woman.

Drake closed out his email and went to join his men. He shouldn't have even stopped to check right before going on a mission, but he'd been curious if Shiloh had messaged him back. Even if Dallas hadn't told him that the woman was upset, her silence would have spoken volumes. He shook the thoughts from his head, trying to focus on the task at hand. An insurgent camp had been located not too far away, and they were being sent to wipe the fuckers out.

He climbed into a Humvee with three of his men and the convoy started the trek through the desert. When they neared their destination, they stopped, hopefully far enough away not to be detected. Jake climbed out of the vehicle and motioned for the men to follow him up the hill. They crouched low and belly-crawled their way to the top. Drake peered through his scope and tried to get a read on the situation.

He counted at least twenty men but knew there had to be more hiding in the tents. It would be fairly even odds, depending on how many were hiding. They'd already discussed the plan of attack at base camp and every soldier knew what was expected of them. Drake gave the signal, and they descended into the camp. The grip on his rifle tightened as their presence was detected. Gunfire rang out, and men on both sides dropped to the sand, their blood tainting the desert.

Drake took down several insurgents as he moved through the camp, looking for the leader. As he approached a tent, a kid not more than fifteen ran out. Drake froze for a second, but it was a second too long. The kid raised his weapon and fired.

Pain exploded through Drake's body as he fell to his knees in the sand. The world spun as his vision dimmed and he collapsed face first. The shouts of the men around him echoed in his ears as he fought to remain conscious. As everything faded to black, the only thing he could think was that he'd never get to know his kid. A woman's face danced behind his closed eyelids. The mother of his supposed child. At that moment, he didn't care much if the kid was really his. If he didn't die in this godforsaken place, he was going to do right by her.

Please, God. If you can hear me, let me make it home.

Chapter Five

Several Weeks Later

Shiloh smoothed a hand over her stomach and the slight flutter she felt there as she stared at the empty nursery. Dallas had worked hard to paint the walls a soft yellow. Rebecca had helped her find an inexpensive bed and changing table at a thrift store. All in all, things were looking up for Shiloh. Her Medicaid card was supposed to arrive in the mail any day, which would finally allow her to see a regular doctor instead of visiting the free clinic, and she'd be able to fill her prescription for prenatal vitamins. If she'd so much as hinted to Dallas or Rebecca that she'd been taking the over-the-counter kind, she knew they would have gotten it filled sooner, but she didn't want to rely on them anymore than she had to.

They had a lot on their minds. Ever since they'd received word that Drake had been injured in combat, Dallas had been on edge. The good news, for Dallas, was that Drake would be returning home soon. Once his doctors declared him recovered enough to make the trip, he would be honorably discharged and allowed to return home. A bullet had nicked his lung and part of the right lung had been removed. While it wouldn't affect his day-to-day life as a civilian, it had been deemed he was no longer suited for combat.

Shiloh would never admit it out loud, but she was a little relieved that he was coming home. She was still seething over his comments about the baby, but she didn't wish him harm. Regardless of how he felt about her pregnancy, he was still her baby's father. The baby fluttered inside of her again and she smiled. The movement was slight, and not something she could feel with her hand yet, but the doctor assured her that would come in time.

Her phone beeped with an incoming text.

Rebecca: Need to see you at the bar.

Shiloh frowned. Since her pregnancy, she'd pretty much avoided the bar. Although, at this time of day, the place wasn't even open. She couldn't think of a single reason why Rebecca would want to meet there. Despite her curiosity, if that was where Rebecca wanted to meet, that was where she would go. She owed so much to Rebecca and Dallas.

Shiloh: On my way

She slipped on the uncomfortable flats and picked up her purse and keys. After locking her door, she carefully walked down the cement steps, wishing she had a railing to grip. She'd had a few dizzy spells the past few days, and she worried she might fall. It took several attempts to close her car door and she locked it as a precaution. With her luck, it would pop open while she was driving like it had the other day. The bar was on the other side of town, but assuming she didn't catch too many lights, she could be there in fifteen minutes. Maybe ten in a more reliable car.

The bar parking lot wasn't as empty as she'd expected when she pulled in. She saw Rebecca's SUV, Dallas's truck, a fancy truck she'd never seen before, and a handful of employee cars. Her curiosity shot up even more as she approached the door. It swung open the moment her hand touched the handle and Rebecca smiled at her broadly.

"I worried I wouldn't be able to get you here." Rebecca tugged her inside and Shiloh's mouth dropped open. "Welcome to your baby shower."

"But how … I never expected anything like this." Her eyes misted with tears. *Stupid pregnancy hormones.*

"Come have a seat," Rebecca said, leading her to

a group of tables that has been pushed together. A pink-and-blue checked crepe tablecloth covered them, and the center pieces were teddy bears holding pastel-colored balloons. There were three bears and each was different.

"You didn't have to do this," Shiloh said.

"Nonsense. You're our friend and we wanted to show our support. When I mentioned a baby shower to Dallas, the girls overheard me and decided it was an excellent idea. You're missed around here."

Shiloh smiled.

"We each brought something to eat," Luanne, one of the waitresses, said. "And of course, you have some gifts."

Shiloh was overwhelmed as she looked around at everything. Someone had hung blue and pink streamers from the ceiling. The length of the bar held an array of food trays and two crockpots, as well as a huge bowl of orange punch and some plastic cups. She hadn't known anyone other than Rebecca cared about her, but it seemed she had more friends than she'd realized.

"I thought we could get something to eat first, then open presents and have cake, and if there's time, I prepared a few games we could play," Rebecca said with a smile.

Shiloh had never been to a baby shower before so she had no idea what kinds of games someone would play, but she'd humor Rebecca and give it a try. Her stomach rumbled, reminding her she hadn't eaten more than a bowl of cereal all day. It was grocery day, but she hadn't made it to the store yet. She really should have gone yesterday, but by the time she got off work, her back was hurting and all she'd wanted was to lie down for a while. Except she hadn't woken back up until morning.

Rebecca handed her a pastel patchwork plate

filled with little smokies, mini croissant sandwiches, crackers with what looked like spinach dip, and mini mac 'n cheese bites. Everything looked good and her stomach rumbled again. Shiloh waited until everyone was seated before she took a bite. Her mouth watered as the tangy sauce from the smokies hit her tongue.

"Eat as much as you want," Starla, another waitress, said. "We brought enough to probably feed twenty people."

"It's really good," Shiloh said between bites.

Conversation flew around the table as everyone ate and drank. By the time they were finished, Shiloh thought she might pop. Rebecca had filled her plate twice more, insisting she eat every bite. If she had one more thing to eat, they were going to have to get a wheelbarrow and roll her out the door.

"Time for presents," Rebecca said with a clap of her hands.

They seated Shiloh at the present table and everyone gathered around her. Several took pictures with their phones as she opened everything. Two packages of diapers, tiny towels and wash cloths, shampoo and lotion, a soft white blanket with yellow ducks on it, and a set of bottles. It was way more than she could have ever hoped for and she fought back tears as she thanked everyone.

"We didn't want to get clothes since you don't know yet what you're having," Rebecca said. "Besides, I think someone else plans to help with that."

Rebecca smiled mysteriously as she looked toward the door. Shiloh followed her gaze and felt her heart drop to her toes. Drake stood uncertainly in the doorway, a bouquet of flowers in his hand. In her alcohol-induced hazed the night they'd created life, she'd forgotten just how gorgeous he was. His hair was buzzed short from being in the military, and he carried himself tall and straight. Broad shoulders filled out his navy polo, and his dark-wash jeans molded to his thighs.

She had to swallow hard as her gaze met his. He stared at her as if he were a starving man and she was the last sandwich, but she didn't understand why. He'd been cruel and cold the only time she'd communicated with him since that night. Why was he here?

"Ladies, I think Drake would like a few minutes alone with Shiloh." Rebecca herded everyone past Drake and out the front door.

He walked toward her slowly and stopped a few feet away, holding out the bouquet as if he were afraid she'd reject the gift.

Shiloh hesitantly reached for the flowers, wrapping her hand around the stems and held them to her nose. They smelled sweet and were the most beautiful thing she'd ever seen. No one had ever given her flowers before, and it was strange that Drake was the first to do so. Maybe under other circumstances it would be different, but she'd thought he hated her.

He motioned to the seat next to her. "Mind if I sit a minute?"

She nudged the chair out with her foot and motioned for him to sit.

"I owe you an apology," Drake said. "When you emailed me about the baby, I didn't react in the best of ways. I can't excuse my behavior, but I wondered if might have a do-over?"

"You thought I was after your money and forcing you to accept another man's baby."

He winced. "In all fairness, I don't know you and you don't know me. I found an alluring woman in my bed that night and took advantage, and for that I'm sorry, but for all I knew I was one in a line of many. Dallas has assured me that isn't the case and said I was an asshole for telling you I wanted a paternity test."

It hurt that he was willing to believe Dallas, and not her, but she had to admit he had a point. Other than their brief moment together, they were strangers. He might know what would make her scream in pleasure, but he knew nothing else about her. She knew quite a bit about him from things Dallas and Rebecca had said, and she had to admit they made him sound like a great guy. Maybe it wouldn't hurt to give him another chance.

"So maybe we should start over," she said. "Thank you for the flowers."

"Have you been to the doctor?" he asked, his gaze dropping to her belly.

"I was waiting on my insurance card to come in the mail before I set an appointment. I went to the free clinic, though, after my home pregnancy test came back positive. They said everything seemed fine."

His brow furrowed. "I'll pay for the visit if you want to set an appointment sooner."

Shiloh shook her head. "From what I've read, I won't be able to find out the sex of the baby for another week or two anyway. I'm only fifteen weeks pregnant. By the time I'm far enough long, I'll find a doctor either here in town or nearby."

His expression was one of awe as he stared at her stomach again. As much as she was enjoying this new side of Drake, she had to wonder what brought it on. It had to be something more than a conversation with his brother. If she was even going to contemplate letting him into her life in any capacity, she had to know that this change was a permanent one. Her hormones were raging out of control and she didn't think she could handle a man with a Jekyll and Hyde personality right now.

"I'm glad you made it home," she said. "Dallas told me about what happened, at least as much as he knew. Everyone was worried about you."

"Even you?" he asked.

She shrugged. "You're the father of my baby, even if you were an ass to me. I never wanted you to get hurt, or worse, not come home at all. I didn't understand why you were so hateful toward me, though. Even if you thought I was just some random woman who had fallen into your bed, I doubt you've treated all of your one-night stands the way you treated me."

"You just caught me at the wrong time. I was half a world away and some woman I'd only met briefly, a woman who had never even given me her name, was claiming that she was pregnant with my kid. You wouldn't be the first woman to try to nab herself a military man by any means necessary, and it rubbed me the wrong way. I'd always thought when I settled down and had kids that it would be with someone I loved, maybe even someone I'd married."

Shiloh nodded. "I never really thought about having kids. I could barely take care of myself, so adding another life into the mix was never on my to-do list."

"Things are okay now though?" he asked.

"I have my own place and a car that gets me where I need to go. I enjoy my job working for Latimer Construction. I may not make as much as I did in tips working at the bar, but I get to work daytime hours and it will be easier to figure out childcare when it's time for me to return to work after the baby gets here."

Shiloh stood and swayed for a moment. Drake jumped to his feet and grabbed her arm, trying to hold her steady. The room spun, but she managed to remain upright. The dizziness was starting to worry her, but she wasn't about to tell anyone else about it. She didn't need Rebecca clucking over her like a mother hen.

"Maybe you should sit back down," Drake said.

"I was going to let Rebecca know it was okay for everyone to come back inside."

"I'll get her. You just sit still for now."

She nearly collapsed onto her seat and watched as Drake cast her a worried glance on his way out the door. When he returned a moment later, no one was following him. She peered around his massive form, expecting the door to open again, but it never did.

"They left," Drake said.

"But we didn't have cake yet."

He smiled. "I'm pretty sure you get to take the cake home with you."

"Yeah, like I need to eat an entire cake by myself." She snorted. "Just because I'm pregnant doesn't mean it's a free license to get fat."

"You're far from fat. If I didn't know you were pregnant, I wouldn't even be able to tell." He frowned. "Shouldn't you be a bit bigger by now?"

"I lost some weight from all the morning sickness the first three months. It's died off now, but I've only been holding food down at every meal for about two weeks. I'm sure I'll start gaining weight now." Provided she could keep her pantry full. Rebecca hadn't stopped back by with more groceries and her paychecks were only stretching so far. She managed to keep sandwich meat and bread in the house, along with milk and a healthy cereal, but things like chicken and pork chops were few and far between.

"You wait here while I load the gifts into your car. Do you want them in the trunk or the backseat?" he asked.

"The trunk doesn't open. Or rather it does, but then it's damn near impossible to close it. The car's unlocked."

His eyebrows rose, but he gathered an armful of

presents and headed for the door, only to return a moment later with a fierce expression on his face. He stopped in front of her with his arms folded over his chest.

"Would you care to explain to me why the only vehicle in the parking lot other than mine or Dallas's happens to be an old beater that should have been removed from the road about fifteen years ago? Tell me you don't seriously drive around town in that thing."

"What's wrong with my car? It might not be pretty, but…"

"It gets you where you want to go," he finished for her. "That car isn't safe, Shiloh. All four tires are bald, and I think one solid bump and the entire thing will fall apart. It's more rust than metal at this point. Don't even get me started on the cracked windshield. How can you possibly see out of that thing?"

She felt her anger burning through her as she shot to her feet. "Just because I'm not rich enough to afford some new fancy car doesn't mean you get to tell me what to do."

His brow puckered. "That didn't even make sense."

"I can't afford a new car, okay? I'm doing the best I can. I have a place that while it isn't flashy, it's clean and keeps the rain out. The baby's room is already set up. Well, the furniture is in place anyway, and Dallas painted the walls for me."

Drake reached for her but pulled his hand back. "I'm sorry. I didn't mean to upset you. I just think the car isn't safe for you or the baby. What if it breaks down on the side of the road at night? Or worse, what if you have a blowout with those bad tires? You could lose control and crash the car. I already checked and there aren't airbags in it."

"I know the car isn't ideal, but it will have to work for now. Maybe by the time the baby gets here I can save a little money and get something better. It still won't be new, but it won't be a death trap either."

He didn't look appeased, but he let the matter drop. Shiloh gathered her things and went out to her car, with Drake right on her heels. She watched as he locked up the bar and gave her a long look before getting into his truck. It was about five minutes down the road before she realized he was following her home. Just what she needed. If he didn't like her car, she couldn't wait to see what he thought of where she lived.

Chapter Six

When his brother had said that Shiloh was struggling, Drake hadn't understood exactly what that meant. Looking at the rusted-out trailer she called home, which matched her rusted car perfectly, he got a sick feeling in his stomach. The cement steps were cracked and the door looked so flimsy a stiff wind would blow it down. The trailer park she'd decided to inhabit was filled with junkies and prostitutes. He might not know Shiloh very well, but he did know that she didn't belong here. The prickly woman wasn't about to accept a handout, though, so he didn't have the first clue how to rectify the situation.

He gathered the things out of her backseat and carried them inside for her. The furniture inside was definitely secondhand, but the place looked clean. Or as clean as it could get. The walls were dark and the carpet was stained, but he could smell whatever cleanser she'd used during her last cleaning spree. A small window unit hummed in the living room, making the room comfortable enough. Pretty soon she wouldn't need one, but he wasn't sure how great the heating unit would be in a place this broken down.

Shiloh motioned for him to follow her down the short hall and she stopped at the first door, pushing it open. The room was a sunny yellow and only held a crib and changing table. This was where she intended for their child to stay? There were no pictures on the walls, no stuffed toys around the room, no rocking chair for her to sit in. It seemed so barren, so sad despite the cheery color. The blinds in the window were torn in places and there weren't any curtains. Seeing how dire her situation was made things more real for him.

"Where do you want this stuff?" he asked.

"You can just put it on the changing table for now. I'll organize it later."

Drake set everything down and surveyed the room again. Just how mad would she be if he took matters into his own hands? If she insisted on living in this place, he could at least make sure his son or daughter had a nice room. It was part of his fatherly duty, wasn't it? Would Shiloh see it that way, though?

"I'm just going to run to the bathroom," Shiloh said. "Make yourself comfortable, or if you have to leave, I'll lock up when I'm done."

She hurried out of the room and he took the opportunity to explore. There was only one other room. Her bedroom. The box springs and mattress were lying on the floor. A dresser missing two drawers took up a small part of one wall. She had a worn-out pair of tennis shoes on the floor at the foot of her bed and the open closet only showed a handful of knit dresses inside. The woman needed help in the worst way, but he had no doubt she'd tell him to fuck off if he offered any.

Before she came back from the bathroom, he hurried into the living room and sat down. The sofa creaked under his weight and he'd have sworn there was a spring poking him in the ass. The longer he was in this place, the more he wanted to scoop her up and carry her off to safety. He'd been raised to respect women, and as archaic as it might sound, he'd been brought up to protect them. Shiloh didn't seem like the type of woman who wanted protection though.

There was a pallor to her face as she sank onto the sofa next to him. She kicked off her shoes and winced as she curled her toes. He didn't know a damn thing about women's shoes, but they didn't look very comfortable. Even his boots had more padding than her flats did. How in the hell was he supposed to get an independent woman to let him help her?

"Have you thought of any names for the baby?" he asked.

Shiloh shook her head. "I decided to wait until I know what I'm having."

"You said you work for Latimer Construction. Why did you stop working for my brother?"

"Dallas fired me when he found out I was pregnant. He said I couldn't work around the smoke anymore. It took me a little bit, but I found a job at the construction company. I just answer phones and handle the filing. It's nice to not be on my feet all the time, but I made more in tips than I do working for Latimer Construction."

Drake frowned. "I know we don't know each other, but that's my kid in there, so if you ever need anything, don't hesitate to ask."

Her eyebrows shot up.

"Let me start over." He held a hand out to her. "I want to get to know you, Shiloh. Will you please let me take you out to dinner tonight? We can go anywhere you'd like. Or if you don't want to go to dinner, then maybe a movie. Or both."

She smiled a little. "You want to take me to dinner and a movie? What is this, a date?"

"What if it was?"

Her smile faltered a little. "Why would you want to take me on a date?"

"Because I want to get to know you. I think it's no secret I think you're beautiful and sexy as hell, but I want to learn more about you. Dallas has talked about you some, but I want firsthand knowledge. We're having a kid together and I think it's important that we form some sort of relationship."

Her shoulders relaxed. "Right. Because you'll be

visiting with the baby and we don't want things to be awkward between us."

Visiting? It didn't feel right that he had to visit his own kid. They'd really fucked up, but Drake knew he'd do whatever it took to make things right. If she only wanted to give him rotating weekends and some days during the week, then he'd accept it. One way or another, he was going to be part of his kid's life. It was going to suck, but they hadn't exactly started things off in a traditional way.

She chewed on her lower lip and he could tell she was thinking hard about it.

"I promise I'm not a bad guy."

"It isn't that. It's just that I like to put on my pajamas on my days off. My clothes are getting snug, except my dresses, but my flats aren't all that comfortable."

He'd figured the shoes were killing her.

"Then why don't we do this instead. You go get your pajamas and anything else you need to get comfortable, and I'll take you back to my place. We can order in or I'll go pick something up and we can stream movies all night. Whenever you're ready to go home, I'll bring you back here, or you can crash at my place."

Her brow furrowed. "Isn't your brother going to be there?"

"He has plans with Rebecca and said he wouldn't be home until late, if at all."

"Where would I stay if I didn't come home?" she asked.

"You can take my bed. I'll crash on the couch."

He could tell she was really thinking about it, and he hoped she'd say yes. Considering they'd already slept together, he didn't think they were moving too fast. It wasn't like he was asking to share the bed with her. He'd sleep better knowing someone was around if she needed help. If something happened to her in this trailer, no one would ever know. Hell, the junkies would probably take advantage of the situation, except she didn't seem to have anything worth stealing.

"What if I decide I want to come home?" she asked.

"Then I'll bring you home, no matter what time it is. I want the chance to get to know you, Shiloh, but I'm not going to make you do something you don't want to do."

"All right. I'll go get my things together."

She stood and walked to the kitchen only to return a moment later with a plastic sack from the grocery store. Did she not even own a tote bag for her things? He'd thought women always had tons of bags and purses. It seemed everything he knew about women he'd have to throw out the window, because none of it fit Shiloh. She was a puzzle and he was determined to figure her out.

When she came back a few minutes later, he escorted her out to his truck and breathed a sigh of relief as he put her trailer in the rearview mirror. How in the hell had Dallas not pushed harder for her to move into the apartment over the bar? With Drake gone and Dallas spending so much time at Rebecca's, it wouldn't have been a hardship for her to be there. Maybe she'd like being at the apartment so much she'd decide to stay.

He pulled into a space at the bar closest to the stairs. Drake wanted to curl his arm around her waist and help her up the stairs, but he wasn't sure his touch would be welcome. He watched her like a hawk until she reached the top. After unlocking the door, he pushed it open and motioned for her to enter first. The lights were already on and the last rays of the day's sunlight drifted through the windows. He was glad he'd taken a moment that morning to pick up a bit. If he'd known that Shiloh was coming over, he'd have put in a little extra effort.

He held out his hand. "If you'll give me your stuff, I'll stick it in my room."

"Would you mind if I took a shower and changed into my pajamas? I know it's still a little early, but…" Her cheeks flushed.

"You don't need to be embarrassed."

"It's just my body is already going through some changes from the pregnancy and my bra is cutting into me. I'm a bit more top heavy than I was before, and from what I've read, it's only going to get worse."

He couldn't help it. His gaze dropped to the breasts in question. Yep, those were definitely larger than he remembered. And fuck if he didn't want to reach out and touch them. It hadn't been lost on him that the last woman he was with was standing right in front of him. Even though he'd been home for several days, and had been hit on multiple times at the bar, he hadn't been the slightest bit tempted. The memory of Shiloh had kept him company at night in Afghanistan, and even now she starred in his fantasies.

"Eyes up here," Shiloh said, pointing to her face.

He smiled a little. "Sorry. For what it's worth, those are rather spectacular even if your bra doesn't fit anymore."

Shiloh shook her head, took her sack from him, and went to the bathroom. He heard the door shut and the lock click. Now he knew where he stood. At ground zero. If he wanted to convince the mother of his child to give him a chance, he was going to have to work hard. He had no idea what to feed a pregnant woman, but he wanted something nicer than pizza or Chinese. Those were the only two options for delivery, unless he could convince someone to pick it up for him.

He shot off a text to Dallas.

Drake: What does Shiloh like to eat?

Dallas: Anything. Seriously.

Drake: If I place an order with The Roadhouse, will you pick it up for me?

Dallas: Why can't you get it yourself?

Drake: At the apartment with Shiloh. Don't want to leave her.

Dallas: I'll head to The Roadhouse in twenty.

Drake smiled and pulled up the number for his favorite steak place. He hoped Shiloh wouldn't be pissed that he ordered without her input, but judging by her car and home, he doubted she had many opportunities for steak and lobster. He was going to spoil her, as much as she would allow. And maybe somewhere along the way, she'd realize he wasn't such a bad guy. If they were going to raise a child together, they needed to get along. But more than that, he wanted an active role in his son's or daughter's life. As in an everyday kind of role. Bleeding all over the sand in Afghanistan, he'd had a moment of clarity. Whatever it took, he was going to show Shiloh just how great they could be together.

He placed their order and paid over the phone. The shower was still running in the bathroom, but he wasn't going to worry just yet. He had no idea what type of movies she liked to watch, but out of the thousands available he was sure that she would find something. He turned on the TV and Blu-ray, and then signed into his Netflix account. If she couldn't find anything there, he'd buy something from Vudu. One way or another, he was going to keep her entertained tonight. Shouldn't be too hard since the only TV he'd seen in her trailer looked like it only had basic cable.

When Dallas dropped off the food and the shower

was still running, Drake decided he'd better check on Shiloh. He knocked, but she didn't answer. Twisting the knob, he remembered it was locked.

"Shiloh, are you okay in there?"

No answer.

He knocked really loud in case she hadn't heard him.

"Shiloh?"

The silence bothered him and he gripped the knob tight, twisting it with such force the lock busted and the door pushed open. His heart hammered in his chest as he slowly opened the curtain, giving her time to scream at him to get out. The breath was knocked from his lungs when he saw her lying in the bottom of the tub. Shutting off the water, he pulled her into his arms and wiped the wet strands of hair back from her face.

"Shiloh? Honey, wake up."

Her face was pale and he checked for a pulse. He found it easily, but he was too rattled to know if it was too fast or too slow. He wrapped a towel around her and carried her to his room, lying her on the bed. Trying to rouse her one more time, he reached for his cell phone. He spoke quickly with the 9-1-1 operator and stayed on the line as she routed an ambulance to him, only leaving Shiloh long enough to open the apartment door.

He stayed by her side until the paramedics arrived and they motioned him out of the way. He watched as they checked her vital signs. Shiloh began to rouse and looked around the room in confusion. When she sat up, her towel dropped to her waist and Drake had to fight the urge to cover her. The paramedics never once looked at her tempting breasts, but it didn't stop his inner caveman from roaring to life.

"What happened?" she asked.

"You passed out in the shower," Drake said.

"I did?" Her brow furrowed.

"Have you had any dizzy spells?" one the paramedics asked. "Any fainting besides tonight?"

"I've been dizzy off and on for about a week, but I've never fainted before now."

"Your blood pressure is a little low. Do you have a regular doctor?" the second paramedic asked.

"Not yet. I was waiting on my insurance card to arrive. I've been to the free clinic though. They said everything was fine with the pregnancy."

"You're pregnant?" the first paramedic asked.

She nodded.

"You should probably ride with us to the hospital so a doctor can check you over and discuss your options."

"I'll be fine," she told him. "I want to stay here."

The paramedics shared a look.

"If she stays here, what signs should I look for?" Drake asked. "I can keep an eye on her."

"If she gets dizzy again, make sure she sits. She may experience some nausea as well. If she's dizzy when sitting or lying down, get her to roll onto her left side. If she experiences a headache, shortness of breath, or starts vomiting, you need to get her to the ER." The paramedic packed up his stuff. "And you can always call us again, but if I come back out here, I won't take no for answer and will take her to the hospital. Dizziness is fairly common in the first and second trimester, but fainting can be dangerous."

"I'll take care of her," Drake promised.

The paramedics left and Drake locked up behind them. When he returned to the bedroom, Shiloh had her back to him as she pulled her pajama top over her head. She'd already pulled on a pair of tiny shorts that hugged her ass in the most tantalizing way. Drake backed out of the room to give her some privacy and decided to set up their food in the living room. Maybe food would make her feel better, even if it wasn't quite as hot anymore.

If nothing else, good food and a good movie would be relaxing for her. Hell, for both of them. His heart was still trying to beat out of his chest. During times of combat he'd been cool and collected. But the moment he found his baby-momma passed out, he freaked the fuck out.

Pussy.

****

Shiloh couldn't believe she'd actually passed out in the shower. She remembered feeling dizzy and then feeling a little faint, but then she didn't remember anything until she woke in Drake's bedroom. It was scary and she was a little worried. If it had happened at her place, no one would have known she needed help. She may have eventually woken on her own, but what if she hadn't? Until now, she'd not been concerned with what might happen if she got hurt, but her visit from the paramedics made her realize that she was jeopardizing the safety of her baby by being so damn stubborn. Rebecca had offered to let her stay at her place, and Dallas had offered to let her stay at the apartment. She'd turned them both down, and now she felt stupid.

When she stepped into the living room, the smell of dinner had her stomach rumbling. Drake was setting their plates and two bottles of water down on the coffee table. She felt a little shaky as she sank onto the sofa. Both plates contained the same meal: steak, baked potato, lobster tail, and a side salad. One steak looked bigger than the other and she assumed the smaller one was hers. Not that she would be able to eat everything on her plate. He must have thought she was carrying triplets.

"You can go ahead and start eating," he said.

"You have to be starving."

"I can wait for you."

He shook his head. "I'm just going to scroll through the new releases and see if anything looks good. We can watch whatever you want."

It had been so long since Shiloh had watched TV that she didn't much care what they watched. She didn't even own a DVD player, and going to the movie theater was out of the question. She was barely scraping by so extras were out of the question.

She took a few hesitant bites of her food and the flavors exploded on her tongue. It had been a long time since she'd had steak and she'd never tried lobster before. Everything was mouthwatering good and before the movie had even started, she was nearly halfway finished with her food. The opening credits started on a romantic comedy she'd wanted to see for a while and she smiled. It seemed Drake knew her better than she'd thought.

After she finished her food, she curled into the corner of the sofa and propped her head on a throw pillow. Drake reached for her, pulling her feet across his lap and he dug into the arches of her feet, giving her the best foot massage she'd ever had. She struggled to stay awake long enough to finish watching the movie, but she didn't quite make it. There was a shift and she felt herself being lifted.

Shiloh opened her eyes. "I can walk."

Drake smiled. "I've got you. Just rest."

She snuggled into him, breathing in his spicy scent. Drake gently laid her on his bed and she blinked up at him sleepily. When he turned to leave, she reached out and grabbed his hand.

"Don't leave."

He hesitantly sat on the edge of the bed. "I'm not

quite sure what you're asking of me, Shiloh."

"I don't want to be alone. Could you sleep in here tonight?"

He smoothed her hair back from her face. "Let me clean up the living room and I'll come back and lie down with you for as long as you want. Okay?"

She nodded and closed her eyes again.

Chapter Seven

Drake watched as the moonlight played across Shiloh's face. She looked so innocent, but he knew there was a strong, determined woman beneath that innocence. He rolled to his side and ran his fingers through her long hair. While he was overseas he'd dreamed so many times of lying in bed with her, and now that he was here, he wanted to savor the moment. No doubt, she'd wake in the morning, thinking this had been a huge mistake. He didn't want to take advantage of her, but when she'd asked him to stay, he'd been powerless to deny her.

He wished they could start over. He'd have done things the right way that night, and would have kept in touch after he'd left. And he sure as hell wouldn't have accused of her pawning another man's baby off on him. It was the one regret he knew he'd always have. Maybe if he'd done things differently, she wouldn't have had to struggle so much, and wouldn't have carried the burden of her pregnancy for so long without confiding in him. She'd fought hard to get where she was, and he wouldn't take that away from her, but he wished like hell she'd admit that she needed help. His help.

Shiloh shifted in her sleep and nuzzled closer to him. Her soft curves pressed against him, making him groan and curse his aching dick. He'd been hard ever since he'd had that first glimpse of her earlier. Not that he was going to act on it. She was the mother of his child, and they were strangers despite their one intimate night together. It didn't mean he wasn't attracted to her, though, and the more he learned about her, the more he wanted her.

His arm tightened around her and he rubbed his chin through her silky hair, his whiskers catching on the soft strands. She felt right lying in his arms, and Drake wondered what it would take to convince her to sleep with him every night. Even if she wasn't ready to take things further, just holding her would be enough. It would give him hope that maybe they could have a future together.

Fuck. He needed his head examined. What the hell was wrong with him? One close encounter and he was ready for wedding bells and baby blankets? Just because the kid was his didn't mean they had to live together. But for some unknown reason, he really wanted to give it a try. The thought of her living in that trailer on the bad side of town made his stomach turn. And his child being brought up there? Hell would freeze over before he let that happen.

Shiloh's hand clutched at his shirt. "You're thinking too hard."

"I didn't mean to wake you."

"I don't sleep the entire night through anyway. I get leg cramps sometimes and have to run to the bathroom other times. If I slept the entire night through, it would be a miracle."

He stroked her arm. "Do you need to get up?"

"I'd better. I'll be back."

She slid out of bed and padded across the hall to the bathroom. Drake folded his hands under his head while he waited. When she cried out, he lurched out of bed and ran across the hall. She was sitting on the toilet with her panties around her knees, but he could see the blood from the doorway. His heart kicked in his chest and there was a roaring in his ears.

"I'm taking you to the ER," he said.

"I need to change."

"Do it quickly. I'll put on some jeans and I'm going to call Dallas to let him know what's going on. I have a feeling he'll want to meet us there."

She nodded as tears streaked her cheeks.

When they were ready to go and his phone call had been placed, he buckled her into the front seat of his truck and hauled ass to the hospital. He screeched to a stop at the ER doors and rushed around to the passenger side to help Shiloh from the vehicle. Drake escorted her inside and left her with a nurse while he went to park. By the time he got back inside, she was speaking to triage.

Drake placed a hand on her shoulder. "I haven't had a chance to add her to my insurance yet, but I'll cover the bill."

She blinked up at him in surprise.

"Drake Edwards?" The nurse's eyes went wide. "I didn't realize you were back home."

His brow furrowed as he tried to place how he knew her, but he came up blank.

"Jeannie Barlow. We met at your bar last year?" Her cheeks pinked. "We had a rather fun night."

He was still drawing a blank.

Shiloh patted his hand. "It's okay, Drake. You have a past. It won't hurt my feelings if you acknowledge her comment."

"I-I'm sorry. Are the two of you married?" the nurse stammered.

"Engaged," Drake said before Shiloh could open her mouth to deny it. "Do you know how long my fiancée will have to wait until she sees a doctor?"

Jeannie looked over the information on the screen in front of her. "Well, because of the pregnancy, she's considered a high risk. I'm going to get an orderly to take her to the back. It's actually been pretty slow tonight, so there are a few rooms open both in the ER and upstairs if they need to move her to the maternity ward."

His heart nearly stopped when he thought about Shiloh losing the baby. He had just gotten used to the idea of being a dad, and he'd hoped things were going well between Shiloh and him. He waited with Shiloh and when an orderly came with a wheelchair to take her into the back, he went with them, hoping she wouldn't kick him out once they reached the room. Drake was every bit as worried as she seemed to be about the baby.

The rooms were curtained-off sick bays and Shiloh stared at him pointedly after the orderly left.

"What?" he asked.

"I'm not changing into that gown," she said, pointing at the garment on the bed, "until you turn your back."

Drake arched a brow. "Really? We're going to pretend I've never seen you naked? Do you need a reminder about *how* you ended up pregnant? Because you certainly didn't get that way by yourself."

She huffed at him and narrowed her eyes, but he wasn't budging. She'd already been unsteady on her feet earlier and now the bleeding had him extra worried. He wasn't going to let her out of his sight for a moment. Hell, if she needed to use the bathroom, he was going there too.

When Shiloh got caught up in her pants and nearly fell, he grabbed her and eased her onto the bed. He helped her get her pants off and then stood back to let her do the rest. She slipped on the gown and he tied it in back for her before helping her lie back on the bed and drawing a sheet over her legs. Drake claimed the chair beside the bed and reached for her hand, giving it a gentle squeeze. There was fear lurking in her eyes and he wished he could put her at ease. The truth was that he was every bit as terrified.

It felt like they waited forever as nurses came in and took her vitals, asked a bunch of questions, and checked on her periodically. When they strapped some sort of monitor to her belly, Drake tensed and wished someone would tell them something useful. The monitor beeped in time to what he assumed was the baby's heartbeat. They spent another two hours at the hospital before they finally got a chance to speak to a doctor.

"I'm Dr. Marks," the man said, holding out his hand to Drake. "The good news is that the baby seems to be doing fine. Some bleeding isn't entirely uncommon, but if it happens again you need to bring her back. I'd suggest that she take it easy for a few days."

"Thank you, Doctor," Shiloh said.

"I'm assuming you two are a couple," the doctor said. "I'd lay off on intimacy for at least three days and make sure you don't start bleeding again. If you feel fine at that point, you're clear to have sex, within reason. No acrobatics or anything kinky."

Shiloh's cheeks flushed and Drake couldn't contain his smile.

The doctor left and a nurse came with Shiloh's discharge papers. While she was getting dressed, he made a payment on her bill with a promise to pay more later. If he didn't get her on his insurance soon, he was going to be broke pretty quick, unless her state-issued insurance card arrived before her next trip to the ER or a doctor.

Drake pulled the truck up to the ER entrance and helped Shiloh into the vehicle. Once she was buckled, he went around to the driver's side and slid behind the wheel. She was silent on the way back to his apartment and he wondered if she was worried about the baby. His fears were momentarily allayed by the doctor, but he knew that anything could go wrong between now and when the baby arrived. He'd just have to keep an eye on Shiloh, as much as she'd allow.

"Thank you," she said softly. "Both for taking me

and for taking on the financial burden of paying for the visit."

"You're welcome. It's my baby just as much as yours. That makes you my responsibility until he or she arrives."

She pressed her lips together.

"I'm glad you were with me when it happened. If you'd been alone at your trailer, what would you have done?" he asked.

"I'm not sure. Tonight has proven that I shouldn't be alone, at least until the baby comes. But Rebecca only has one bedroom, and you don't exactly have space either."

"Staying in my room wasn't so bad tonight, was it?" Drake asked. "There's no reason we can't share a bed until the baby gets here. If you don't want me to touch you, I'll keep my hands to myself."

She stared at him. "Is that what you want?"

Should he tell her the truth, or lie his ass off?

"You've been different today. In your email, you were hateful and nasty, but you've been the perfect gentleman since you walked into the bar today. I'm not sure which is the true Drake. The guy I've seen today I wouldn't mind being around, but the one who sent that horrible email? That guy I could do without." She licked her lips. "If today has been a glimpse of who you really are, then maybe us getting to know one another wouldn't be such a bad idea. We're going to have a kid together, and even if we're not a real couple, we're still going to have to deal with each other all the time."

"Would being a couple really be a bad thing? Like you said, we're having a kid together. I'm sure people have gotten together for worse reasons."

"You're kidding, right? Today is the first time we've had a real conversation or spent any time together, other than when the baby was created. You don't honestly expect me to rush into a relationship with you, do you?"

"Would it be rushing? We only have so much time between now and when junior gets here."

"Really? All you know about me is that I'm broke, carrying your kid, and your brother is my friend. And you want to talk about happily-ever-after with me?"

Okay, so maybe she had a point. He might be rushing things because of the baby, and in all honesty, if there wasn't a baby, he wouldn't even be thinking about asking her to live with him. Maybe even marry him. If she wanted to slow things down, then he'd do that, but damned if he didn't want her under his roof while they got to know one another. Just the thought of her being alone and falling in her trailer with no one around to help, gave him chills.

"All right, we'll go slow." He glanced her way. "I swear I'll keep my hands to myself if you'll agree to stay with me. And if you really want your space, we can see if Dallas will temporarily move in with Rebecca and you can have his room."

"I'm not throwing your brother out of his apartment. We can share the bed."

She didn't look too thrilled with the idea and Drake wanted to kick his own ass. If he hadn't sent that nasty email to her, then they wouldn't be in this predicament. They could have talked in the last few weeks and gotten to know one another.

"FUBAR," he muttered.

"What?" Shiloh asked.

"Nothing." It was accurate, though. He'd definitely fucked up the situation beyond all recognition. He wasn't entirely certain how to dig his way out of the very deep hole he'd dug for himself, but he was determined that Shiloh would welcome his company by the time the baby arrived.

Way to go, asshole. Your baby momma can't stand you.

Whatever it took, he was going to make Shiloh see she could depend on him. Even if it took the remainder of her pregnancy to do it.

Chapter Eight

Shiloh sat at her desk the following Wednesday, staring at her computer screen. Her mind had only half been on her job since she'd moved in with Drake, even if it was just temporary. At least, she'd told herself it was temporary, but paying four hundred a month for a place where she wasn't even visiting was a little ridiculous. He'd asked her to stay with him, but if she gave up her place, where would she live after the baby was born? It wasn't like they were a couple and would be living together indefinitely.

She gathered the files on her desk and put them in the appropriate drawer of the filing cabinet. When she turned back around, she was greeted by the most beautiful bouquet she'd ever seen. There had to be at least two dozen brightly colored blossoms dripping from the crystal vase.

"Are you Shiloh Anderson?" the delivery guy asked.

"Yes."

"I just need you to sign here," he said, holding out a clipboard.

She signed her name and handed it back, and then reached for the card nestled in the flowers.

Beautiful flowers for a beautiful woman. —Drake

"As if flowers solve everything," she muttered. She stuck her nose in the blooms and inhaled, admitting they were gorgeous and smelled divine. He'd been doing his best to prove he wasn't a complete asshole, and she had to admit her resolve was starting to crumble—a little.

Charlie stepped into the room and his eyebrows rose. "Is Sergeant Edwards still trying to win you over?"

"Something like that." No, it was exactly like that. While she'd enjoyed the expensive dinners and pretty flowers, they weren't enough to make her commit to a relationship she wasn't sure would last. Pretty words and fancy things meant he had the means to take care of her and a baby, but she worried in the end her heart would get trampled.

"I'm going to be out of town the next few days, so I wanted to make sure I gave you your check." He handed it over. "You've been working hard lately so I added a little extra. I know you will refuse to accept it, but put it toward stuff for the baby. You can never have too many diapers."

"Thank you, Charlie." She slid the check into her purse after a cursory glance. He'd added more than "a little", but she wasn't going to point that out.

"I'm going to leave a little early today so I can go home and pack. If you'd like, you can have the rest of the afternoon off. I won't dock your pay. Just turn on the voicemail service before you leave. When you come in the next two days, you shouldn't have much to do but answer the phone. If you want to bring a book to read, I'm fine with that."

"Are you going somewhere fun?" she asked.

"I've been promising the wife a tropical vacation. We're going to Hawaii for four days. We leave first thing in the morning and won't return until Sunday night, so I may be a little late on Monday."

Shiloh smiled. "I hope you have a nice time."

"You have my cell phone if an emergency crops up. My foreman should be able to handle anything on the jobsite, and any new business that comes through can wait until my return. Just explain that I'm out of the office until lunch on Monday. That will give me time to come in and get caught up before the phone starts ringing off the hook."

"I'll take care of it."

"Now, get your stuff and get the heck out of here." He smiled. "Time for you to enjoy life a little. I'm sure that Sergeant Edwards wouldn't mind a little extra time with you. Just remember, make him work for it. Don't be afraid to be demanding with the man, Shiloh. If you want something, tell him."

Relationship advice from her boss? Although, the man had been married a long time so he probably knew what he was talking about. She smiled and nodded before setting the voicemail and gathering her things. She headed out to her rust bucket of a car and had to admit that an afternoon off sounded great. Mostly because she'd love to get out of her miserable flats. He'd told her jeans were fine, but she didn't want to push it by wearing her ratty tennis shoes too. If she had a new pair though … she thought about the check in her purse. Maybe spending a little of the extra on a pair of shoes wouldn't be such a bad idea. They didn't have to be expensive, but it had been a long time since she'd bought a brand-new pair. Most of her stuff was secondhand.

She stopped by the bank on her way home and deposited her check, and then drove straight to the apartment. There were several boxes on the steps and Dallas was loading more into the back of his truck. She parked and got out, wondering what was going on. He'd talked about moving in with Rebecca, but she hadn't realized it was a done deal.

"Moving day?" she asked.

Dallas grinned as he glanced her way. "Yeah. It was supposed to be a surprise when you got home tonight, but it seems you're early. Drake wanted to take you baby-furniture shopping and turn my room into a nursery. He's already in there painting it yellow like the one at your place. Don't worry, he left the windows open so the fumes wouldn't bother you."

"But I have a bed and changing table."

Dallas gave her a pointed look.

"And he wants brand-new stuff, doesn't he?" She sighed. "I guess if he wants to spend his money on something we don't have to have then that's up to him."

"You realize you just said 'we'? You thinking about his offer of moving into the apartment permanently?"

"I don't know. If I'm going to be here for the duration of my pregnancy, it doesn't make much sense to keep paying for the trailer. Storing my furniture somewhere would be cheaper. And then after the baby comes I can look for a new place. Maybe I can save some money between now and then and get a nicer place."

"Or maybe you use that money for a better car," a voice said behind her.

She turned to look at Drake, biting her lip so she wouldn't laugh at the smears of yellow paint on his face and bare chest. "You know, you're supposed to paint the wall, not yourself."

"I'm multi-talented and can do both at the same time."

Dallas snorted. "Did you get it on the floor too?"

"About that… I was thinking now would be an excellent time to put in wood floors, or at least that laminate stuff. It's easier to clean with a baby on the way, and it won't stain like carpet. I could do one room at a time during the days Shiloh is at work, or maybe on the weekends she could hang out with Rebecca while I do another room." He grinned. "And the carpet in the nursery is now specked with yellow and has one long smear along one wall."

Dallas rolled his eyes.

"Or I could stay at my trailer while you do that," she said.

Both men scowled at her.

"Or not." She sighed. "If you're redoing the floors in the bathroom and kitchen too, we might have to stay elsewhere while you finish your project. You'll have to pull the appliances out of the kitchen."

"She has a point," Dallas said. "I'll be the first to admit the apartment needs an overhaul, and if you're going to be painting, she doesn't need to be around the fumes. I say y'all pack some bags and get a suite at the Magnolia Lodge."

"Cheaper is fine," Shiloh said, knowing full well a suite at that place would cost almost two hundred a night. No sense spending that kind of money if they didn't have to.

"I've never before met a woman who didn't like to spend money," Drake said. "Not to worry, sweetheart. I get a family discount and we can more than afford to stay there. I didn't really touch my money during my deployments so all that combat pay has been stacking up in the bank."

"Doesn't mean you have to blow it on a fancy hotel room." Shiloh placed her hands on her hips. "I will be perfectly fine sleeping in a Sleepy Daze Motel room. Or is that not ritzy enough for you?"

Drake rolled his eyes. "Fine, Scrooge, we'll get a room at the Sleepy Daze Motel. I don't think it will take more than week to renovate this place."

"Why don't you repaint the whole place?" Dallas asked. "You could let Shiloh pick the colors. I'm sure she has better taste than you."

Drake groaned. "Thanks, bro. Any other work you want me to do?"

"Not like you're doing anything while she's at work anyway. When are you going to stop being a bum and get a job?"

"Thought I had one at the bar."

"Nope, I'm full up. You'll still get your cut as part owner, but you need something to do to keep you occupied. Get this renovation out of the way and then seriously look for something to do. You won't be able to live off your savings and the pittance from the bar forever. Especially with a baby on the way."

"I'll make some calls in a week or two. I think I've earned a little downtime. Besides, the lung isn't completely healed yet."

"Should you be breathing in paint fumes?" Shiloh asked. "That can't be good for you."

"She has a point. Why don't you hire a contractor? Hell, have him do the entire renovation. It will give you more time to focus on Shiloh."

She cast a glare at Dallas. She had more than enough of Drake's attention as it was. The last thing she needed was him being more focused on her.

"Speaking of being focused on me…" She turned to face Drake. "Thank you for the flowers. They were beautiful. I decided to leave them at the office until I come home Friday so I can enjoy them while I'm there."

He grinned like he'd just won the lotto and smoothed a hand down his abs. Hardly fair, since it just drew her attention to his incredible body. He wasn't shy about flaunting it, and had even "accidentally" forgotten his clean clothes while showering so he could parade around the apartment in a towel—which had also "accidentally" slipped a time or two. He was shameless, and she had to admit she loved every moment of it. Except for the part where it left her horny and she was determined not to act on her growing desire for the hunky Sergeant.

"I'll just throw on a shirt and pack a bag for us. We can go to the motel tonight and I'll come back tomorrow for more of our things. Anything in particular you want for work tomorrow?" he asked.

"No. Jeans and a nice shirt will be fine." Her cheeks flushed as she thought about him handling her undergarments. Not because she didn't want his hands on them, but because they were a little on the threadbare side. Some of her panties even had holes in them. Her wardrobe needed an overhaul in the worst way.

Drake took off up the stairs while Dallas finished loading his truck. The heat made sweat bead on her lip and her hair stick to her neck. By the time Drake made another appearance, she thought she might melt into the parking lot. He tossed a large bag into the back of his truck and motioned for her to get in.

"I need my car," she said.

"No, you don't. I'll take you to work and pick you up. Maybe by the time the week is over, I'll convince you to give that rusted heap a proper burial in the junkyard. I'm not sure they'll even accept it as scrap."

"Picking on my car is not winning you any points with me."

His eyebrows went up and he pointed at her car. "That is not a car. It's a death trap."

"He has a point," Dallas said. "You should make Mr. Moneybags over there buy you a new one."

"He's not buying me a car."

"Fine," Dallas said. "He can buy the baby a car and you'll just have to drive it for the next eighteen years."

"Not helping," she sang out.

"Get in the truck, Shiloh," Drake said. "We can argue about your sorry excuse for a car later. Right now, I want a shower and some air conditioning. I don't want to discuss much of anything until then, and I know you have to be miserable in this heat."

He had her there. With a sigh, she got in his truck and slammed the door, giving him a mutinous look as she buckled her seatbelt. Drake just shook his head and pulled out of the parking lot. The Sleepy Daze Motel was on the other side of town. Not in a horrible area, but certainly not the upscale part of town either. It looked respectable enough when they pulled into the parking lot. She followed Drake inside and checked out the lobby. The furniture was worn but clean, and everything smelled springtime fresh. An older lady was working the counter and smiled broadly at them.

"Welcome to the Sleepy Daze Motel. How long will you be staying with us?"

"About a week," Drake said. "We're doing renovations on our apartment so I'm not sure of the exact checkout date."

"We have plenty of room for the next few weeks so that won't be a problem at all. All of our rooms come with a king-size bed and are equipped with a microwave, coffeepot, and small fridge. There should be a few bags of complimentary coffee in your room, enough to make one pot per bag. If you run out, just let me know and I'll get some more for you."

King-size bed. As in one bed in the room? Shiloh nearly groaned. She'd been sharing a bed with Drake for nearly a week, but she'd hoped to put things back on even footing by having her own bed. Maybe she should have let him splurge on the more expensive place after all. Being spooned by him every night, those strong arms wrapped around her, was hell on her resolve. She wanted him, but she didn't want to want him.

The woman got Drake's information and credit card and then handed him a keycard, and another for Shiloh. He ushered her back outside and they got back in the truck and pulled around to their room, parking right outside the door. Drake retrieved the bag out of the back of the truck and unlocked the motel room door. The inside wasn't as bad as Shiloh had thought it would be. Anything was an improvement over her trailer, but she'd been a little worried that Drake would take one look at the place and bolt.

"See, not so bad," she said as she smoothed a hand over the blue comforter.

The walls were a taupe color and the carpet on the floor looked almost new. There was a table with two chairs and an armchair in the large room. It was far more spacious than she'd thought it would be. Overall, it was a typical motel room, just a lot cleaner and nicer than what she'd anticipated from a place called Sleepy Daze.

"Honey, I've slept in sand in the middle of the desert. I wasn't getting a room at the Magnolia for me. I was getting it for you."

She had to admit she melted a little. He was always thinking about her. Part of her wanted to rage at him to stop being so damn nice to her all the time, and the other part … the other part liked that a guy was trying to treat her right. It was just so damn hard to let him do everything for her when she'd had to stand on her own two feet for so long. Even when she'd been with her ex, she'd had to fight for everything she had. Life had been hard for Shiloh, and she was worried that if she gave in and Drake got what he wanted, that she'd get used to having an easier life and one day she'd wake up and it would all be gone.

Drake tossed their bag on the dresser and pulled out some clean clothes. With a wink, he disappeared into the bathroom. She heard the shower turn on and rolled her eyes when she saw the bathroom door standing wide open. Did he think she was going to strip down and join him or something? She wasn't sure if she wanted to laugh or be mad at him. Laughter won out when he started singing White Town's "Your Woman" at the top of his lungs. For a soldier and cowboy, the man sure did love his nineties music.

While Drake cleaned up, she propped herself up in bed and turned on the TV. No Netflix, no Blu-ray player. But they did have some movie channels. It wasn't like she spent a huge amount of time watching TV, but it was nice to know she had options. Oh hell. He probably didn't pack any of her books and she was going to need at least two for tomorrow. She thought about that extra money she'd put in the bank and wondered if Drake would take her shopping. If they went to the big box store, she could get a new pair of shoes and a few books. The rest of the extra money could go toward things for the baby, but she didn't think she'd make it much longer with her uncomfortable flats.

Drake came out a short while later, toweling his hair dry. She wasn't sure if she was relieved he had already dressed, or disappointed. He seemed to read her thoughts and grinned like an idiot before tossing the towel back into the bathroom.

"So, what should we do with your free afternoon?" he asked.

"I need to do a little shopping."

"Like mall shopping or around town shopping?"

"Like Wally World shopping."

"Not that I have anything against that store, but what if we drove over to Buffalo Gap and hit the Target over there? They carry maternity clothes, and you'll need some before too long. Might as well have a few things ready."

He made a good point, even if that store was a little more expensive. Maybe she'd get lucky and she'd find some shoes on clearance while she was there. She nodded and got off the bed, rubbing her aching lower back. Her belly wasn't big enough yet for the pregnancy to be causing her aches and pains, but poor footwear was a definite possibility.

Shiloh knew there was no point in arguing with Drake, so they went to Buffalo Gap. The first stop in the store was to get a package of socks and then on to the shoe department. They had several pairs of tennis shoes on clearance and a few sandals. Drake talked her into getting one of each, then he tossed a pair of bedazzled house slippers into the cart. She started to point out that she didn't need them in the summer, but his look quelled her argument. At the rate they were going, she would blow through her extra cash and everything would be for her.

He led her over to the maternity department and helped her pick out a few outfits. When she tried them on, she had to admit they were far more comfortable than her regular jeans, and it made her realize her baby belly was showing more than she'd thought. Once he knew her size, Drake threw several pair of maternity jeans into the cart along with a handful of shirts. She was about to stop him from adding anything else when he tossed in three pairs of shorts. As much as she wanted to keep her costs down, she agreed that shorts were reasonable with their scorching hot summer.

"Drake, I can't afford all this," she said as he threw in a swimsuit that she was certain she would never wear. "I only needed one pair of shoes and maybe a few books."

"We're getting everything you need, and if you think I'm letting you pay for this, you're crazy. Just because you're too stubborn to agree you're mine doesn't mean I can't take care of you." He placed a hand over her bump. "That's my baby incubating in there. You're going to be miserable enough being pregnant in this Texas heat, the least I can do is try to make you more comfortable."

"Drake, you aren't responsible for me. I understand if you want to help with the baby, but this is going overboard."

"Do you know what I hear every time you argue with me?"

"I'm scared to ask," she muttered.

"I hear 'kiss me, Drake'."

Shiloh rolled her eyes and followed him as he went over to the intimates area. She stared at him as he pawed through bras and panties, adding more stuff to the cart. At this rate, he was going to give her an entire new wardrobe from the skin out, which was beyond ridiculous. She didn't have a clue what his checking account looked like, but this was certainly going to put a dent in it. She bit down on her tongue to keep from saying anything as he moved along to another department. When they finally checked out up front, the total came to a staggering five hundred dollars and change.

"Drake, you can't…"

"Shush, woman. I'm taking care of you and that's final."

"But, Drake, this stuff is crazy expensive."

He dug through his wallet and handed her a bank receipt. The fact he'd pulled out several hundred dollars would have been shocking enough, but the balance showing at the bottom nearly dropped her to her knees. How in the hell had he managed to save over one-hundred grand on a soldier's pay? Shiloh had never seen so much money before and felt a little faint.

Drake took the slip back from her and finished

paying for their purchases. He pushed the overflowing cart out to his truck and Shiloh helped him load everything into the backseat. While he put the cart up, she got in the truck and buckled. She'd known he had more money than her, but knowing he could give her a baby a life she'd never dreamed of…she didn't know what to do with that information. Ever since he'd come back it had been her intention to make sure he saw the baby as much as he wanted, but would he settle for that?

Thinking of her rusty trailer and the old baby bed and changing table nearly made her cry. Having learned more about Drake Edwards over the last week, she knew there was no way he'd let her raise a baby in a place like that. And if she wanted to fight him for custody, he'd be able to hire a good lawyer while she'd have to find someone who would work pro bono. She didn't have a prayer of hanging onto the little life growing inside of her, not if Drake decided he wanted full custody.

"You look a little green," he said as he got into the truck. "Do you need something to eat or drink?"

"I'm fine."

But she wasn't. Worry ate at her on the way back to the motel. Drake had told her several times he wanted her to move in with him permanently, and she knew it was because of the baby, but she was starting to question if maybe he was right. If she did move in with him on a permanent basis, then they would both get to see the baby every day. But could she live with a man who didn't love her?

Drake insisted she go into their room and lie down while he unloaded everything. Kicking off her shoes, she stretched out on the bed and sighed in relief. When the last of the bags were brought in, he shut the door and flipped the chain across the top. Drake pulled off his boots and lay down next to her, turning on his side so he could look at her. With a gentle touch, he reached out and brushed her hair away from her face.

"Need a nap before we discuss dinner?" he asked.

"I'm always hungry, but sleep sounds really good right now. Shopping was exhausting." She bit her lip. "Thank you for all of my things."

"You're welcome." He smiled a little. "I like it when you let me take care of you. And before you puff up and tell me that you can do everything on your own, I'm well aware that you're capable of taking care of yourself. I admire everything you've done since being dumped at the bar, but letting someone help you doesn't mean you're weak."

"I'm not used to relying on other people. Even when I was with my ex, I was still responsible for my own stuff. We didn't have a joint account or anything, and we split all the bills, except for things that we didn't share. Like his Xbox Live account. He paid for that, and I paid for my bookstore discount membership."

His lips twitched as he fought not to smile bigger. "You really love books, don't you?"

She nodded.

"How many do you read in a week?"

"I don't know. It depends on the week, but maybe ten or so? I don't really keep track. I get most of my books secondhand or at library sales. The Gulch Springs Public Library had a sale last month and I was able to buy an entire sack of books for five dollars. I went through them pretty quick though."

"So, the handful we picked up today will only get you through to the weekend?"

"Maybe through Saturday."

"Do you only read romances?" he asked.

"I prefer them, but I've been known to pick up a mystery here and there. I really love the ghost hunting mystery books. And I've been known to read some of the young adult books too. I devoured *Twilight* when it came out."

"The one with the sparkly vampires?"

"Why do you make it sound dumb? Edward was hot."

He laughed and shook his head.

"So, what do you read?" she asked.

"I like westerns. Don't get me wrong, I like other books too, but that's the genre I keep going back to."

Her brow furrowed. "You mean like that show *Longmire*?"

"Exactly like that."

"I guess I can see the appeal."

Drake reached and traced the line of her nose before leaning over and lightly brushing his lips against hers. It was the first time he'd tried to kiss her since coming back home and it startled her. She looked up at him with wide eyes, but when he leaned down a second time, she didn't stop him. His lips were warm against hers. His kiss was gentle and tentative, as if he was afraid she'd pull away at any moment.

He stared into her eyes and caressed her cheek with his thumb. "I know you think I'm only paying attention to you because of the baby, and I admit it started out that way, but I genuinely like you, Shiloh. I'd really like it if you'd give us a chance. I'm not perfect, and I don't claim to have all the answers, but I'd be good to you."

"You already are."

"So, will you? Give us a chance? I'm not asking you to walk down the aisle with me, and even if we start dating, it doesn't mean I expect you to wear my ring at some point. If you just want to live together, I'm okay with that."

"You'd be okay with us cohabitating without a legal commitment? You won't try to claim we're married by Common Law?"

He smiled. "You have my word. And in Texas, you'd have to agree to marry me and tell people you're my wife in order for Common Law to apply. It's not as simple as just living together. If all you want is a boyfriend, then I promise to be the best boyfriend you ever had."

"I'll think about it."

"That's all I ask. Get some sleep, Shiloh. We'll grab dinner when you wake up."

He kissed her softly again, and then turned onto his back and turned the TV on low. He'd given her a lot to think about, but she had to admit his proposal was intriguing.

Damn the man. Could he have possibly been more perfect?

Chapter Nine

Drake hated that Shiloh felt cornered, and he knew she did. He'd seen the look in her eyes every time he'd mentioned them living together. Last night, she'd finally agreed to think about it, but he worried for every two steps forward he might have to take three steps back. He'd read some pregnancy books and learned about nesting. It was his hope that the apartment renovation would trigger Shiloh's nesting instincts and she'd make the place her own. He'd already hired someone to rip out the carpet and linoleum. The laminate and ceramic tile was already on order. In hindsight, he should have let her pick it, but he hadn't wanted to wait until she was off work.

With the renovation taken care of, he had too much free time on his hands. Dallas was right. He did need a job. They could live comfortably for quite a while on what he had stashed in his bank account, but he'd be bored out of his mind. It had been rough this past week, staying home while Shiloh went to work. His brother slept all day since he worked all night. But what the hell kind of job could he get? It wasn't like his skills were required in civilian life. Not that he was sorry he'd joined the Army. He'd learned a lot, and, thank God, he hadn't come home with PTSD.

He'd retrieved his laptop from the apartment when he'd met with the contractor and opened it to browse his options. It was doubtful there were many jobs open in Gulch Springs. Their tiny town didn't have much, but it had always been home. Drake remembered having to drive to another town just to grocery shop when he was little. Then more people started moving in, stores started popping up, and before long they were booming. Well, as booming as a small town could get.

They'd never be the size of Dallas, and he was glad of it.

While he was right about Gulch Springs not having much, Buffalo Gap was another matter. It was only twenty minutes up the road, so working there wouldn't be so bad. He'd known several guys in the Army who got out and went to work for their local police departments. He wondered what Shiloh would think about him wearing a gun and a badge. Then he thought about putting his life in danger every time he went to work, and realized he didn't want to put his family through that. His son or daughter should never have to wonder if Daddy was coming home.

"What the fuck am I supposed to do with my life?"

He snapped the computer shut and leaned back in the chair. He couldn't be a soldier anymore, and wouldn't have re-upped if even if he hadn't been discharged. What kind of safe, respectable job could he possibly get that he would be proud of, that his family could be proud of? The VA hospital was too far away or he'd volunteer until he figured things out. Maybe he could find work doing something with his hands? Painting was out until his lung fully healed. He was passable at carpentry, but he didn't know if he wanted to do that every day.

He felt completely useless. Most of the jobs nearby didn't require a college degree, which he didn't have, but they did require some experience. He didn't think they would care much that he knew how to take out insurgents. Drake got up and snatched his keys off the dresser and then went out to his truck and drove around town. As a kid, he remembered some of the locals posting job ads on the library bulletin board. At this point, he'd try anything. It wasn't so much that he needed a job right this minute, but … yeah, he pretty much did need a job right now or he'd go stir crazy sitting on his ass.

The library parking lot was full and he had to park nearly half a block away. When he stepped inside, he saw why. The place was crawling with small kids and their moms. A large, glittery sign announced story time was about to start. He managed to maneuver through the chaos to the bulletin board on the far wall. It was mostly sales flyers and ads for babysitting, but there were a handful of job announcements. One in particular caught his attention.

Part-Time Ranch Hand Wanted. Must be able to rope and ride. Work hours will be 5:00 AM to 2:00 PM Monday through Thursday. $400 per week. May become full-time in the spring.

Drake copied the man's name and number into his phone and hoped he hadn't found someone already. He might not have ridden much in the last ten years, but he'd grown up riding and roping. He'd even competed in some rodeos during high school. It might not qualify him to be a ranch hand, but it never hurt to give the man a call and see what he said. Maybe he'd give Drake a chance to prove himself.

When he got back out to his truck, he turned on the air conditioning full blast and gave the guy a call.

"Buckhorn Ranch," a man said.

"I'm calling about the ad posted at the library for a part-time ranch hand."

"Do you have any previous experience?"

Drake told him about his rodeo experience and all the summers he'd ridden at his grandparents' farm. He admitted that he hadn't ridden in the last ten years and explained why. The man's tone changed almost immediately.

"Thank you for your service, son. Tell you what.

Why don't you come out here tomorrow for a tryout? Say around nine o'clock? I should be free by then to see what you've got. My name's Hank and you can find me at the front barn most days."

"I'll be there, and thank you, sir."

Drake smiled as he hung up. It wasn't a done deal, but he planned to wow the man tomorrow. He just hoped like hell he remembered how to rope. Riding wasn't a problem. Riding a horse was like riding a bike, except his ass was going to be sore the first week on the job. He hadn't thought to ask if he'd need his own saddle. He could buy one, if he needed to, but no sense spending the money before he was sure.

The clock on his dashboard said it was 12:15 and he cursed. Shiloh was probably starving and wondering where the hell he was. He'd promised to take her to lunch at twelve, and even though he wasn't overly late, he'd always prided himself on being punctual. Leaving the mother of his child to go hungry was a shit thing to do, even if it had been unintentional. When he pulled into a spot at Latimer Construction, Shiloh was waiting at the edge of the makeshift parking lot. She didn't look pissed, just tired.

When she climbed into the truck, he leaned over and kissed her cheek. "I'm sorry I'm late. I was job hunting and time got away from me."

"Find anything?"

"Maybe. I have a tryout of sorts at a ranch just outside the town limits. It's just part-time to start, but the ad said it could become full-time in the spring. Or maybe I'll like part-time and just stick with those hours if he'll let me."

She frowned a little. "Can we make it if you only work part-time? I mean long-term. I only make about three hundred a week after taxes. Less once I start paying for health insurance."

He liked that she'd said "we." Maybe she was seriously considering his offer.

"We'll be fine. Ranch hands make pretty good money, even part-time. I kind of like the idea of having more time with the baby. We'll still need to figure out childcare for the mornings once you go back to work."

"Sounds like you've thought of everything."

"Is there anything in particular you'd like to eat for lunch? Any special cravings?"

She smiled a little. "I haven't really had cravings. Even the morning sickness isn't as bad anymore. I'm hoping the rest of the pregnancy will go smoothly."

"You'd tell me if you were still having dizzy spells, wouldn't you?"

"Probably not. You worry enough as it is. As long as I stay upright, that's all that matters. You heard the EMT, he said that some dizziness was to be expected. I'm eating better, I'm getting plenty of rest, and the doctor at the hospital said the baby was fine."

He couldn't help but worry about her. It was obvious she hadn't been doing a very good job of taking care of herself. She'd had so little that it was hard not to want to spoil her some. The apartment they were sharing was small, and as their son or daughter grew they were definitely going to need more space, but he was going to make it as homey as possible for her. He figured they could stay there at least another year, maybe two, before he'd need to seriously think about getting a house. Kids should have a yard to play in, not a bar parking lot.

Since she didn't tell him where she wanted to eat, he drove to the diner. He'd noticed she was partial to their apple pie. She didn't complain when he pulled into a space near the door. They went inside and found a booth near the window. The sunlight played over her hair, making it shine like a sunset. He didn't understand how she'd been single all the months she'd been in town. Couldn't everyone see how beautiful she was, not only on the outside but on the inside as well? Sure, she fought with him like a rabid possum when she felt he was overstepping, but he'd seen the kindness she showed everyone on a regular basis—even to him.

"You're staring," she said. "Do I have something on my nose?"

"No. Just thinking about how beautiful you are," he answered honestly.

She blushed and looked down at her menu. The woman didn't know how to take a compliment and he wondered if maybe there had just been too few of them in her life. Whatever asshole she'd dated before, the one who had dumped her here, should be taken out and flogged to within an inch of his life. How anyone could mistreat her, he didn't know. Every time he thought about that hateful email he'd sent her, shame burned through him. She had every right to hold it against him, and he didn't blame her one bit, but he hoped she was learning he wasn't the asshole she'd professed him to be.

They ordered their food and Shiloh stared out the window, her lips tipped down at the corners as if something heavy weighed on her mind. He wished that she'd talk to him, unload her burdens. He wanted to help her and not just financially. How could he make her see that he wanted to be there for her in every way? To support her emotionally as well. He'd bought her flowers, treated her to nice dinners, even taken her to a movie. And still she kept herself apart from him. Except for when she slept … at night she curled into his arms and seemed content to be with him.

Maybe he wasn't thinking big enough, or perhaps he'd been thinking too big. Flowers and dinners were great, but they weren't very personal. If he showed her that he paid attention, that he knew what she loved and hated, perhaps he could convince her he was in this for the long haul. And not just for the baby, but for her too. Christ! If his Army buddies knew the shit going through his head, all over a woman, he'd never hear the end of it. He was supposed to be a battle-hardened warrior and here he was having an internal mope fest because Shiloh was being difficult. Women really did make men stupid.

They ordered their food and he continued to get the silent treatment. She barely even touched her sweet tea, and he knew how much she loved it. She'd been fine when she'd left for work that morning, and he didn't the news of his possible job would have upset her so much. That only left work…

"Why were you standing at the edge of the parking lot when I pulled up?" he asked. It had been odd and he'd just thought her anxious for lunch, but now he wondered if there was something more to it.

"No reason." She wouldn't meet his gaze.

"Shiloh, did something happen at work today?"

"It's nothing. I'm sure I'm overreacting."

He reached out and placed a hand over hers, drawing her attention his way. "If something happened, you can tell me."

Her eyes filled with tears and he immediately felt like a jerk for pushing her. He squeezed her hand but had no idea if he should hold her or stay where he was. She brushed the tears from her cheeks with her free hand and sniffled.

"Charlie is out of town until Monday, and he left orders for me while he was gone. I thought I could handle it, that everything would be fine, but … I hadn't counted on the construction workers."

"Didn't he leave a foreman in charge of them?"

"Yes, but…"

"Sweetheart, whatever it is, just spit it out. Maybe it's not as bad as you think. Sometimes you just need another person's perspective on something."

"One of the men came into the trailer before lunch. I was up from my desk and filing something when I felt someone behind me." Her tear-filled eyes focused on his. "He slammed me against the filing cabinets and tried to pull up my skirt."

"Shiloh, did he…" Drake swallowed the knot in his throat. "Did he hurt you, baby?"

"He bruised me a little and he tried to tear my panties, but I managed to catch him by surprise and kneed him in the crotch. It gave me enough time to get out of the trailer. I went down to the parking lot, hoping you were there."

Drake got up and went around to her side. He sat and pulled her into his arms. "I'm so sorry, sweetheart. After lunch, I'm going to have a talk with the foreman and then I'm taking you home. And don't argue. I'd rather know you're safe than take a chance on something happening to you while Mr. Latimer is away."

"I didn't know what to do," she said as she buried her face in his chest.

"Do you feel up to talking to the police? He shouldn't get away with it. He was going to rape you, honey, and he's likely tried with other women."

"If you're with me, I'll talk to them."

"We'll stop by on the way home. I don't want you going back to work until Mr. Latimer returns. If you have his number, you can call him from home to tell him why you aren't there."

She looked up at him. "You don't think he'll be mad I'm not at the office?"

"No, I don't. I think he's going to be pissed at the

worker who tried to hurt you."

Their food arrived and Drake convinced Shiloh to eat. It both infuriated and sickened him that something like that had happened at her work. She should be safe in her workplace, and he was going to make sure nothing like that ever happened again. If Latimer couldn't guarantee her safety, then he'd convince her to quit. They'd manage somehow.

At the construction site, Shiloh was too scared to get out of the truck. She told Drake the name of the man who had hurt her and he promised to take care of it. Drake went into her office to gather her purse and lock the door then he went in search of the foreman. An older man with a weathered face was barking orders to everyone. Drake waited to get his attention and then asked him to step aside, out of the hearing of the other workers. He doubted Shiloh wanted everyone to know what had almost happened to her, even though it hadn't been her fault in the least.

"You have a worker here named Richard Martin," Drake said. "I wanted to give you a heads up that the police will be having a word with him."

The foreman shook his head. "What's that hot head done now?"

"He tried to rape Shiloh in the trailer before lunch. She's in my truck, refusing to step foot on the construction site. I'm taking her to the police station to file a report and then I'm taking her home, where she'll stay until Mr. Latimer returns."

"Fuck!" The foreman looked out over his crew. "Tell her I'm real sorry about what happened. Man to man, though, I've always thought there was something off about that guy. I've kept him on because he's a good worker, but now I'm wishing I'd let him go and gone with my instincts."

"So, we aren't going to have a problem?"

"No, and I don't blame you one bit for keeping her home. I won't say or do anything until the police arrive so he's not tipped off. Once he's off the grounds, I'll call Mr. Latimer and let him know what happened. Shiloh going to be okay?"

"She's shaken up, but she'll be fine. I don't know how much she's going to trust your men after this though."

"Take care of her. She's a sweet thing and I hate that this happened."

Drake shook the man's hand and went back to Shiloh. She was chewing on her bottom lip as he slid behind the steering wheel. He reached over and took her hand, giving it a squeeze, before kissing her cheek. If she'd had trouble telling him what happened, he had a feeling things weren't going to go very smoothly at the police station. He hoped she didn't change her mind about filing a report. He'd once read an article that said oftentimes when a woman was raped or nearly raped they blamed themselves for the incident. No one should ever go through something so horrific and think it was their fault. Some people were just born wrong.

"I can't claim to understand what you went through," Drake said, "but I want you to know that I'm here for you. You don't have to face it alone."

"I keep thinking I must have done something to make him think that was okay. Maybe my dresses were too short or shirts too low cut. Did I flirt with him and not realize it?"

"Honey, no. This isn't your fault. You didn't do anything wrong."

Tears started slipping down her cheeks again. "Then why did he do that to me? What made him think that was okay?"

"Baby, he didn't care if it was okay or not. He's a sick man who likes to hurt other people. It didn't have anything to do with the way you dressed or how you talked to him. Something isn't right in his mind."

She nodded and held his hand tightly.

"Come on. Let's go talk to the police so I can get you home. I'll run you a bath and you can relax the rest of the day. You can either lounge in bed and read, or if you want to go do something I'll take you wherever you want to go."

"A bath sounds nice."

"Everything is going to be okay, Shiloh. I won't let anything happen to you."

She gripped his hand tight and nodded as she stared out the window. He didn't know how long it would take for her to feel safe again, but he was going to do whatever it took to see that man brought to justice. He hoped it would be enough to at least give her closure. No one deserved to go through what Shiloh had been through, but he thanked God the man hadn't gotten any further. If anything had happened to her … well, anything worse. Thankfully, she was just frightened and had gotten away. But if she hadn't … he might have been going to jail tonight because he would have beaten the hell out of that guy.

Chapter Ten

Shiloh swirled her hand through the water in the motel tub. Talking to the police hadn't been fun. Despite Drake's words of comfort, assuring her she'd done nothing wrong, the police had practically grilled her about what happened, making her feel like she was the one at fault. Drake had told them to back off or they were leaving. It had taken nearly an hour to get the report filed and an assurance that the matter would be handled. She didn't quite know what that meant. Were the police going to talk to him and give him a slap on the wrist, or were they going to arrest him? She didn't know what she'd do if he still worked at the construction site.

Drake knocked on the bathroom door. "Everything okay in there?"

She stared at her pruning fingers. "I'm fine. I'll be out in a minute."

The water was turning cold anyway. She drained the tub and got out, drying off with the scratchy towel. Shiloh pulled on a clean pair of panties and some new pajamas Drake had bought her, and then she stepped out into the motel room, the carpet cool under her bare feet. Drake had the air conditioner blasting and the room held a nice chill compared to the oppressive heat outside. Summer in Texas was no joke.

Drake sat on the foot of the bed, flipping through channels on the TV. He looked up as she got closer and abruptly stood. His hands clenched at his sides and there was a look of concern on his face. Shiloh stepped closer and wrapped her arms around his waist, pressing her cheek against his chest. His arms came around her and she felt his lips brush the top of her hair. It was comforting, being in his embrace. Strange since she'd fought so hard to keep her distance, and yet when something bad happened, the first person she'd wanted to see was Drake. Maybe her resistance hadn't been so much about Drake, but about her fear that yet another man would run out on her.

"Do you want to lie down? Or do you want to sit up and read for a while?" Drake asked. "You can pick whatever you want on TV, but there's not much on."

"Can we lie down and watch a movie? I don't care what it is."

"We can do whatever you want, Shiloh. I know it's still early, but whenever you're ready for dinner, I'll have something delivered. I'm afraid our options will be Chinese or pizza." He rubbed her back. "Or if there's something in particular you want, I can either run pick it up or ask Dallas to drop it off."

"I'll think about it. Right now, I just want you to hold me."

"I can do that."

Shiloh pulled out of his embrace and pulled back the covers on the bed. Slipping beneath them, she waited for Drake to remove his boots and jeans before he slid into the bed with her. She cuddled against his side with his arm around her and stared blankly at the TV. Today had been a really close call, and while she knew most of the guys at the construction site were good men, she wasn't sure how safe she felt there anymore. But what else could she do? If Drake was only working part-time, they'd never make it on just his salary, even if they apartment was rent free.

"Your phone rang while you were in the tub," Drake said. "I hope you don't mind, but I answered when I saw it was your boss calling."

"Does he know?"

"Yeah, baby, he knows. He said that if that man wasn't arrested, he'd make sure he was fired first thing in the morning. He agreed you should stay home until he's back in the office and he said he would pay you for the days off. He plans to be in the office at eight o'clock on Monday so he said come in any time after that."

"What if he goes out of town again?" she asked. "Or what if he has to leave the office and I'm there alone? How do I know I'm safe there?"

"He said the two of you would discuss things when he got back. He was concerned about you and I'm sure he's going to come up with some precautions so it doesn't happen again."

She nodded and cuddled a little closer.

"Shiloh, if you don't feel safe there anymore, I'm sure he'd understand if you want to find another job. No one will think badly of you."

"I looked for two weeks for a job before I found this one. No one would give me a chance except Mr. Latimer. I like doing office work, even if it didn't pay as much as waitressing at the bar. And who is going to give me a shot when I'll be out on maternity leave in about six months?"

"You have my support no matter what you decide."

Shiloh had never backed down from a challenge, and she doubted she would start now. Yes, she was scared about what could happen if Mr. Latimer wasn't around, but it wasn't like her to run away from her problems. She'd meet with him Monday and see what he had to say. If nothing else, she'd keep working there until she could find something else. But she really liked her job and hoped everything would work out.

She must have dozed off at some point during the movie because the next time she blinked at the screen the credits were rolling. A peek a Drake showed that he was still awake. She shifted against him and sat up, rubbing the sleep from her eyes. He gave her a smile when he saw she was up and reached out to smooth her hair down.

"Have a good nap?" he asked.

"How long was I out?"

"About an hour. It's nearly four now so we still have a little time before dinner. Unless you're hungry?" he asked.

Truthfully, she could eat, but that was only because she normally had a snack at her desk around this time every day. They'd purchased some bananas and apples at the store yesterday, so she got up to get one. As she munched on the banana, she slid back into bed and leaned against the headboard.

Drake smiled. "If you were hungry, we could have gone ahead and ordered."

"I'm fine," she said between bites. "It's my snack time."

"When I agreed to stay in a motel with you for a week, I never realized how boring it would be here. You have to be tired of regular TV by now, even if we do have some movie channels."

"At the trailer, I either watched basic TV or read a book when I wasn't working. It was nice having Netflix and the apartment, but I don't need it to survive." She smiled. "I'm fine just spending time with you."

He cursed. "I have that meeting tomorrow at the ranch. Maybe I should reschedule. I don't like leaving you here alone."

"Could I come with you?" she asked.

"I don't suppose it would be a problem. It's a tryout for a job, but if I explain what happened today, I think it would be okay for you to be there. Are you sure you don't want to sleep in?"

"I'm sure." She smiled. "I think I'd like to see you in cowboy mode."

Drake laughed. "All right."

"If I put some clothes on, do you think we could go out to eat and maybe stop for ice cream after?"

"Are you sure you're up to going out? I'll take you wherever you want to go, but maybe you should rest."

"I'm fine, Drake. Honest. If something happens and I feel like being out is more than I can handle, then I'll let you know and we can come back here. But I can't hide in this motel room until Monday when I return to work."

"Let me get my jeans and boots back on and we'll head out. If you're hungry now… Or do you want to wait a little?"

"If we go now, we can beat the dinner crowd."

Drake kissed her cheek. "Then get ready and we'll head out."

It didn't take long for Shiloh to pull on a pair of shorts and a t-shirt. She slipped on the flip-flops Drake had bought for her and then she ran a brush through her hair. By the time she was done, Drake was ready to go. Shiloh wasn't sure what she wanted to eat, so Drake drove the main strip until something sounded good. They ate at Lola's, even though neither was dressed for it. Shiloh was amazed they weren't turned away at the door.

"What do you want to do tomorrow when we're finished at the ranch?" Drake asked as he dug into his meal.

"I've heard there's a wildlife park nearby. Could we maybe do that?"

"Sure. I haven't been there in a long time."

"What do you normally do for fun?" she asked.

"I haven't had many friends around town since I joined the military, so I usually just hang out with Dallas or do stuff on my own."

"And apparently take random women to bed," she said with a hint of a smile. "I still can't believe you didn't remember that nurse."

He winced.

"Have there been so many you can't remember them all?"

"I never forgot you," he said quietly. "When I was over there, not knowing if I'd make it home or not, you were the one I thought of to get me through. I remember my night with you and how sweet you'd looked the next morning. And I'd mentally kick my ass for not waking you up and kissing you goodbye."

She melted a little at his words. "Really?"

He nodded.

"I thought about you too, even before I knew I was pregnant. And then I found out about the baby and I figured you wouldn't want either of us. I didn't know what to do."

"And I acted like an ass when you reached out. I'm so sorry for that email, Shiloh."

"It's in the past. I probably could have handled things better too. We're both at fault, but the important thing is that we put it behind us and move forward." She twirled her fork through her pasta. "Thank you for being there for me today. I know I've kind of frozen you out lately and I'm sorry. I thought it was because I was still mad about the email, but it's not. I think deep down I'm worried that you'll be like all the others and bail at the first opportunity."

"Shiloh, I would never abandon you and our child."

"I know. Now."

"Does this mean you're open to the idea of dating me? Maybe taking things to the next step whenever you're ready?"

"I'm already living with you. What next step could we have?"

He stared at her quietly a moment. "You could marry me."

Her fork clattered to her place. "Are you proposing?"

"Maybe."

"Either you are or you aren't."

"All right. I am. Will you marry me, Shiloh? I don't have a fancy ring for you, and I'm sure you've always dreamed of some romantic proposal, but it's heartfelt. I want us to be a family."

"We can be a family without marriage," she pointed out.

"Fine. I want you to be mine. I want a ring on your finger that shows all the assholes out there that you belong to me."

"Is this about earlier?"

"No. But I have to wonder if you were married if he'd have tried anything. He'd have known there was a guy who would beat the shit out of him for touching you."

Shiloh took a sip of her drink as she contemplated what to say. She loved that he wanted to marry her, that he was willing to make things more than just temporary between them, but was she ready for that? While she'd come to grips with the fact he was a good man, a worthy man, and she should give him an honest chance, she didn't know if jumping straight to marriage was the answer.

"How long of an engagement are we talking about?" she finally asked. "Because if you plan to whisk me off to the courthouse come Monday, you'd better think again."

"I'd like to have the wedding before the baby gets

here."

"Drake, I … I'm flattered that you want to marry me, but I think I need a little time to think it over. I'm not saying no, just not right this minute. Are you okay with that?"

He smiled. "You take as much time as you want. The fact you aren't saying a definite no gives me hope."

They finished their meal and then walked along Main Street, peeking in at the different shop windows. She dragged Drake into an antique shop and they browsed the different booths. It wasn't until she wanted to show him a booth filled with books that she realized he wasn't right behind her anymore. The store wasn't very large and she found him easily enough. There was a secretive smile on his face as he paid for something at the register. It was something small judging by the size of the paper sack the woman handed him.

"See anything you want?" he asked.

"There's a booth filled with books, but before I could look at them I realized you weren't with me and came to find you."

"Just doing a little shopping."

They walked back around to the book booth and Shiloh grabbed a handful. After they paid, Drake took her hand and led her back to the truck where they dropped off their packages. The ice cream shop was a few doors down on the opposite side of the street, so they walked over. Shiloh thought it was nice getting to hang out with Drake and to do things normal couples do. Even when she'd first started dating her ex, she hadn't had as much fun as she did with Drake. It didn't have anything to do with money, and everything to do with the kind of man he was.

By the time they got to the motel room, Shiloh was ready to change back into her pajamas. The flip-flops weren't uncomfortable, but her feet were a little swollen. They'd picked up her mail on the way to dinner and her insurance card had arrived. She didn't know how long it would take to get an appointment with a doctor, but she hoped she could get in soon. From what she'd read, if she had an ultrasound now, they would be able to tell the sex of the baby. It would be nice to be able to pick out a name.

Drake parked outside of the motel room door and helped her out of the truck. He swiped the keycard and let her go in first. The icy air was welcome after being out in the heat. It left goose bumps along her arms as she put down her sack of books. Whatever Drake had purchased, he tucked into the front pocket of the duffle bag. It was tempting to ask what he'd bought, but she'd let him keep his secrets.

Drake brushed a kiss on the top of her head after he'd pulled out a pair of loose shorts. "I'm going to take a shower, unless you want to get in?"

She shook her head. "You go ahead."

When the bathroom door clicked shut, she pulled out her pajamas and let her dress fall to the floor. As she reached for the fastener on her bra, the bathroom door swung open and Drake stepped out. He froze as he saw her semi-dressed and she couldn't miss the heat in his eyes.

"I, uh…" He rubbed the back of his neck.

"Did you forget something?"

"I was going to charge my phone. When I pulled it out of my pocket, I realized it was on two percent."

Feeling bolder than she was, she walked over and held out her hand. "I'll charge it for you."

Drake handed it over but couldn't seem to tear his gaze away from her. Her stomach was a little rounder than usual, but not by much. Her breasts were another matter … now much fuller than before. Her nipples pebbled against the lace cups of her bra. Drake groaned and took a hasty step back. The look on his face clearly said he wanted her, but she could see the inner fight as he tried to be a gentleman and walk away.

Except she wasn't sure that was what she wanted. "Drake?"

Her gaze lifted to hers.

"What if I don't want to shower before you… What if I want to shower *with* you?"

"Shiloh, you can't say things like that. I'm trying really damn hard to give you space."

She closed the gap between them and placed her hand on his chest. "I don't want space anymore."

"If we do this, if we take this step, I won't be able to stay away from you. Once you're in my arms, I'm not letting you go. I was an idiot to walk away before, but I won't this time. Waking up every morning with you in my arms has shown me what I want … I want you. I want to wake up with you every morning and fall asleep with you every night. I want to fill you so deep that neither of us can tell where one of us stops and the other starts. I want you screaming my name and coming apart in my arms."

Her breath hitched in her throat.

"And if you can't handle that, if you aren't ready for that, you need to get as far away from me as possible right now, because I'm holding on by a thread."

"I want you, Drake. I've thought about night together often, and I want to feel that way again. No one has ever made me come as hard as you did. When you touch me, it's like every part of me comes alive."

He growled softly and hauled her tight against his body before slamming his mouth down on hers. Her heart raced as his tongue delved between her lips, tasting and teasing. Desire blazed in his eyes as he pulled back and looked down at her, giving her one last chance to move away. She clung to him tighter and willingly followed as he dragged her into the bathroom. The calluses on his fingers rubbed against her skin as he divested her of her bra and panties. His gaze darkened when he saw she'd shaved and was completely bare.

She shivered as she waited for him to strip, taking in every inch of skin he exposed. His cock was hard and it twitched as she stared at it. Her mouth watered just thinking about having a taste of him.

She didn't remember him being so big, but if he'd fit once, he'd fit again. Drake helped her into the shower, the warm water hitting her skin and soaking her hair. He followed behind her and pulled the curtain closed. A breeze wafted around the corners, making her nipples even harder. He cupped her breasts and teased the hardened tips as he kissed her so thoroughly she thought she might melt.

"So, beautiful," he murmured against her lips. "If you change your mind, if you want to stop at any time, tell me."

"Don't stop. Please don't stop."

There was a hint of concern in his eyes and she knew he was thinking about the incident at work. While she'd been frightened, she knew it was Drake touching her, and she knew he'd never hurt her. Shiloh reached out and wrapped her fingers around his cock, stroking him hesitantly at first then firmer. He bucked against her hand and she knew she had to have him.

Shiloh dropped to her knees and licked her lips. She swiped her tongue across the head of his cock, lapping up the pre-cum that had beaded along his slit. He tasted salty, but good. Her lips fit around him, her tongue stroking the underside as she took as much of him as she could. Drake reached for her, his fingers sifting through the wet strands of her hair. He didn't grab her, or force his cock down her throat. He just held her as if she were the most precious thing to him.

When he erupted, shouting out his release, she swallowed as much as she could and then licked her lips to get the rest. Drake braced a hand on the wall as she panted for breath, reaching down to help her stand. Her knees ached from the hard tub, but she couldn't complain. Drake wrapped his arms around her, scorching her with his kiss. He didn't seem to mind that she tasted of him as he devoured her mouth, as if he couldn't get enough of her. Shiloh thought they would wash and get out when he drew back, but instead he fell to his knees and braced her against the wall.

Shiloh's legs parted and his breath fanned against her sensitive skin. He lapped at her silken lips before drawing her clit into his mouth. She sank her fingers into his hair and let the sensations roll over her. Every nerve in her body had come alive as his masterful lips and tongue took her to heaven not once but twice. Drake stood and turned her to face the wall. His lips traced along her shoulder as his hands caressed her hips. Need surged through her.

"Spread your legs, baby, and let me in."

Shiloh spread her legs as far as the tub would allow and pressed back against him. She felt the head of his cock sliding against her folds, and then he was pushing inside, stretching her in the most delicious way. She'd expected a hard, fast pounding, but he took his time, as if he were savoring the moment. Every stroke made her pussy clench and her breath catch. As Drake caressed her, whispered filthy things in her ear, and sent her to heights she'd never experienced, his name sprang to her lips. Her release left her breathless and seeing stars as Drake stroked in and out of her, his thrusts becoming harder and faster until he came inside her.

Drake wrapped his arms around her waist and held her close as he peppered her neck and shoulders with kisses. "You are absolutely incredible."

"Is every time with you going to be amazing?"

"I hope so."

Drake pulled out and turned her to face him. He tipped up her chin and kissed her softly. With infinite tenderness, he washed her hair and body before quickly washing himself. Shiloh was almost afraid to blink in case he disappeared. Did men really act the way Drake did? She'd never met anyone like him before. To say she'd always attracted assholes would be an understatement. They got out of the shower, and she dried off and put her pajamas on. Drake went to the bed and pulled the covers back.

"What are you doing?" Shiloh asked.

"Going to bed."

She pointed at his still semi-erect cock. "You're naked."

"I like to sleep in the nude, and since you're not avoiding me now, there's no point in dressing for bed."

Shiloh put her hands on her hips. "Are you going to take care of midnight diaper changes naked too? What if we have a little girl? She doesn't need to see that!"

Drake smirked. "I'm pretty sure I won't scar her for life when she's an infant. But if it makes you feel better, I'll put on underwear before I change any diapers."

Shiloh shook her head and climbed into bed. So, what if he wanted to sleep naked? It only meant that hard, naked body would be pressed against her all night. Maybe she should even the score and rip off her pajamas before getting into bed. He looked so relaxed with his hands folded behind his head as he watched whatever was playing on TV. It would serve him right if he had to sleep with a hard-on. She toyed with the hem of her tank before ripping it over her head.

"What are you doing?" Drake asked, his eyes wide.

"Getting comfortable. If you can sleep naked, so can I."

"Um, no you can't."

She arched a brow. "Watch me."

She shimmied out of her shorts and panties before slipping under the covers. It didn't escape her attention that there was a tent forming over his body. With a smug smile, she flicked off her light and got comfortable in the bed.

She felt the bed shift as Drake rolled onto his side. A rough palm slid up her thigh, over her hip, and cupped her breast.

"Didn't you get enough in the shower?" she asked, smiling in the darkness.

"I can never get enough of you."

She shifted so that she was rubbing against his cock. His hips bucked until his shaft was rubbing between her ass cheeks, and a shiver went through her. No one had ever taken her there, and she wondered if one day Drake would. She doubted it would be tonight, since they weren't prepared, but it was something to fantasize about.

"You want me, don't you, Shiloh?" His teeth nipped her earlobe. "You want to feel my monster cock sliding deep inside you, fucking you until you can't walk. Isn't that what you want?"

She whimpered.

"Tell me it's what you want, baby. Tell me you want me to fuck you."

"Yes," she cried. "Yes, I want you to fuck me."

Drake rolled her onto her back and pinned her to the mattress. "I'm going to spend the rest of the night making sure you know you're mine, that you're wanted."

His words sent a thrill through her. Yes, she was his. And she wondered if maybe she'd been his since their first night together. Her body responded to his touch as he set her aflame, pushing her desire to the breaking point. As his lips claimed hers, Shiloh felt like she'd come home.

Chapter Eleven

Drake shifted in the saddle, the leather creaking under his weight. He tightened his gloved hands on the lariat as he watched the herd. He'd thought being back in the saddle would feel awkward, but it felt completely natural. His thighs and ass might not think so later though. Even though he couldn't see Shiloh where she stood at the railing behind him, he felt her gaze. Probably trained on his wranglers, he thought with a smirk. They'd stopped by the apartment on the way to the ranch to pick up his cowboy hat and she hadn't taken her eyes off him yet. If he'd known it only took some tight jeans and a Stetson, he'd have dressed this way sooner.

The other guys on the ranch had been reserved, until they'd seen he was able to saddle a horse on his own. Hank had introduced him to the team he'd be working with during his tryout. They seemed like a good group of guys. At the moment, they were hanging back to give him room to work. The saddle creaked under him again as he shifted his weight, watching the herd. It had been so long since he'd been on a working ranch, but it felt good to be back in the saddle. It was peaceful even if it was hotter than hades. Ranching was hard work, rain or shine, but he was willing to put in the hours. He took a cleansing breath of the hot, humid air, holding it in his lungs a moment. After being in the desert, this was like heaven.

Bessie, the ranch's cattle dog, cut a heifer from the herd. As with any good cow pony, his horse knew what to do without much prodding. He twirled the lariat over his head before letting it sail through the air. He looped the heifer and wound the lariat around the saddle horn as the beast struggled. He'd been told it was a catch-and-release scenario, so he climbed off his horse and let the cow go.

Hank spat on the ground near his feet. "Well, you can rope, and it seems you can ride. How handy are you at mending fence line?"

Drake smiled and climbed back onto his horse. "I can hammer and nail with the best of them."

"You can start Monday. There's a thirty-day probationary period. If you're doing a good job at that point, we'll consider the job permanent." Hank nodded toward Shiloh. "Might want to leave her home next week. She seems the type that has to touch every furry beast she comes across. Some out here aren't so friendly."

"She is that. Don't worry, she has her own job to get to. She's just off a few days while her boss is out of town. With her being pregnant, I don't like to leave her alone for too long. I won't make it a practice of bringing her to work with me."

"Well, Sergeant Edwards, I'll see you bright and early Monday. Best get that horse rubbed down and put up so you can take your wife home."

He didn't correct the man. Shiloh might not be his wife, but she was the mother of his child and that was every bit as precious. Drake swung his leg over the back of the horse and gathered the reins in his hand. Pulling off his work gloves, he shoved them into his back pocket. After leading the gelding back to the barn, he unsaddled the horse, rubbed him down, and put him back in his stall. Shiloh hung back, but watched his every move. He felt the absurd urge to flex while he was working, just to see if he could get her to lick her lips like she had when he'd put on his hat. He couldn't remember the last time he'd been so entertained by a woman.

He shut the gate on the stall and flashed her a smile. "You ready to get some lunch?"

"That was kind of hot," she said.

"Which part?'"

"All of it."

Drake laughed and took her hand, leading her to the truck. "Does this mean you have a thing for cowboys now? And here I thought you were more of a soldier groupie."

"Honestly? I was too busy checking out your ass to look at any of the others."

"Careful or I'll find a place where you can show me just how much you like my ass." He winked and helped her into the truck. Brushing a kiss against her cheek, he fastened her seatbelt. "I think my baby deserves the biggest piece of peach pie at the diner."

She sighed and rubbed her belly. "You know all the right things to say."

Drake chuckled and shut her door. As he climbed into the driver's side, he couldn't help but smile. Life was looking up. He had a baby on the way, a sweet woman in his bed, and he now had a job that he was convinced he would love. As far as Drake was concerned, life couldn't get much sweeter.

He shot off a text to his brother on the way to the diner. As much as he loved the one-on-one time with Shiloh, he figured she'd probably like to see Dallas and Rebecca. And maybe having his brother as an audience would keep him from groping Shiloh under the table. Ever since he'd had a taste of her, he'd wanted more. They'd hardly gotten any sleep last night, but it had been well worth it. There was nothing hotter than her screaming his name as she came apart in his arms.

He pulled into a space at the diner and helped Shiloh out of the truck, placing an arm around her waist as they walked inside. Dallas and Rebecca were already seated in a booth by the window. Shiloh lit up when she saw them and he ushered her into the booth before sliding in beside her.

"How's this asshole treating you?" Dallas asked Shiloh as he pointed at Drake.

"Things are good," she said, a blush staining her cheeks.

"Ah ha! It looks like the two of you kissed and made up." Dallas smirked. "I knew you wouldn't be able to hold out for long. He always did have a way with the ladies."

Rebecca elbowed him. "Shut it."

"What?" Dallas asked, rubbing his ribs. "What'd I say?"

"Like she needs a reminder of his reputation," Rebecca said.

"Anyone with eyes can see he doesn't want anyone but her," Dallas argued. "Besides, they're cute together."

Drake shook his head and handed Shiloh a menu. "Get whatever you want."

"You're trying to make me fat," Shiloh grumbled. "Pretty soon I'll be as big as a house. You won't fit in the apartment with me."

"I'll build him a doghouse in the parking lot," Dallas offered.

"Just think," Rebecca said. "After this baby, you'll be a pro when the next one comes."

Shiloh shook her head. "One baby. I never wanted to tackle motherhood. And now that it's here I wouldn't wish it away, but I don't think I want another one."

"How do you feel about that?" Rebecca asked Drake.

"I never really thought about being a dad, so it doesn't bother me if we only have one kid. One kid or a dozen, I think in a few years I'd like to look at buying a house. Somewhere with a yard."

Shiloh looked at him. "How are we going to afford a house?"

"Let me worry about that."

"What about Grandpa's land?" Dallas asked. "It's just sitting there unused."

"What land?" Rebecca asked.

"Grandpa had a ranch and then he had several plots of land around town and outside the city limits. He was always buying up acreage when it popped up. The ranch was sold, along with quite a bit of the land, but that corner lot at Maple and Vine belongs to us," Dallas said.

"I figured you'd build a house there when you settled down," Drake said.

"I think I'd rather claim the ten acres outside of town if you're okay with that," Dallas said. "Rebecca would like to open a pet sanctuary and it would give us some space for a barn and a kennel."

"I didn't know you did animal rescue," Shiloh said.

Rebecca nodded. "I help at the shelter a few days a week and I foster when I can. I try not to keep them very long though because I'm afraid I'll get attached and not want to let them go."

"I've never had a pet before," Shiloh said. "I wonder how one would react to a baby."

Drake rubbed her thigh. "Do you want a pet? I don't think the apartment is big enough for something large, but maybe a cat or a small dog?"

"Wouldn't it be mean to make a dog live somewhere without a yard?" she asked. "And I'm not sure a cat would be good with a baby. Maybe we should wait a few years."

No, if Shiloh wanted a pet, he'd damn well get

her one. A small dog really wasn't a bad idea. It would give her a companion if he had to work on her days off, and it would alert her in case of trouble. While it was true they didn't have a yard, there was a strip of land behind the bar that was part of the property. At one point, Dallas had thought of expanding the parking lot, but they could easily walk a dog there for now.

The waitress came and took their order, apologizing for the wait. She promised their food would be up soon and then hurried off only to return a few minutes with later with drinks.

Drake shared a look with his brother, and he knew Dallas was on the same page. Dallas gave him a nod. While the women chatted, Drake plotted of ways to get Shiloh the pet she wanted. He knew the shelter had reasonable rates, and he'd much rather rescue someone in need of a home than purchase a puppy from a breeder.

"I forgot about an errand I need to run," Drake said. "Can Shiloh hang out with y'all for a little while? I'll swing by and pick her up when I'm done."

"Can't you just take me to the motel?" Shiloh asked. "My feet are kind of swollen and I'd like to stretch out for a while."

Drake frowned. "Are you all right? If you're uncomfortable, we could get our food to go."

"I'll be fine long enough to sit here and eat."

"When are you going to see the doctor?" Rebecca asked. "Didn't your insurance card come in the mail?"

"It did. I have to find out which doctors around here will take it though. Not everyone accepts the state's insurance plan. Being a new patient, I'm sure I'll have to wait a few weeks." Shiloh smiled. "It's all right. By the time I'm able to see someone, I should be able to find out if I'm having a girl or boy, so it will be worth the wait."

"I'll call Doctor Thompson this afternoon," Drake

said. "I bet we can get you in to see him tomorrow. And if you need to go back later for an ultrasound, then I'll see that you get there. I know you don't want to take off work if you don't have to, but you have to stay healthy."

She rolled her eyes. "Yeah, and that slice of peach pie I ordered was really healthy."

Dallas snorted. "Well, it has fruit in it. It's not like you ordered the chocolate mousse pie."

Shiloh groaned. "That sounds really good too. Maybe I could get a slice to go."

Rebecca smiled. "I'm glad you got over your independence enough to let Drake pay for your meals. It was really hard for us to watch you struggle. I think my heart broke when I dropped off those groceries and saw how bare your kitchen was."

Shiloh's cheeks flushed as Drake eyed her. "Something you want to tell me?"

Rebecca's softly spoken "oops" made Shiloh wince.

"Were you going hungry?" Drake asked.

"Money was tight. I wasn't starving."

"She was living off ramen and canned pasta," Rebecca said. "And I think there was a package of hot dogs in the fridge."

"And I blew you off when you needed help the most." Drake groaned. "You had every right to think I was an asshole. I could kick my ass for treating you that way. Maybe if I'd been more open to the idea of you being pregnant, then you might have confided in me and I could have made sure you were taken care of."

"Drake, I'm a big girl and can take care of myself. I was struggling, and things were pretty bad, but I had a roof over my head, transportation, and while the food in the pantry wasn't stellar at least there was something to eat." Shiloh shrugged. "I've been in worse situations."

His gut churned as he thought about how bad things had been for her. It made him even more determined to give her anything she wanted or needed. While he'd been half a world away, pissed that someone was trying to foist a baby off on him, she'd been fighting to survive. It had never occurred to him that she reached out because she needed help. He'd just assumed she wanted a free ride.

"You really were an asshole," Rebecca said.

"I think he's beating himself up enough," Dallas said. "No need to rub it in. He fucked up and he knows it. Question is how he's going to rectify the situation."

"Guys, I'm fine. I was fine and will continue to be fine. I've decided to live with Drake even after the baby comes. If we stay in the apartment, we don't have to worry about rent and with both of us working things should be fine. My days of struggling are over, but even if something happens, I know I can get through it." Shiloh nudged Drake. "And if he turns into an asshole again, I'll just throw him out of the apartment and claim it as my own."

Rebecca laughed until she snorted. "And she'd do it too! You'd better watch out, Drake."

"If I screw up that bad, she's welcome to the apartment," Drake said.

Their food arrived and Drake kept an eye on Shiloh, looking for any sign that might need to go back to the motel. She might have said she was fine, but he knew she'd push herself until she passed out. When they were finished, and had paid the check, Drake helped Shiloh into his truck. If she wanted to go to the motel, he'd take her. He just wished she'd agreed to hang out with Dallas and Rebecca until he was finished.

"I won't be long," he told her as he opened the

motel room door. "You call me if you need anything."

"I'll be fine, Drake."

He kissed her softly before closing the motel room door. As he backed out of the parking space, he saw her peeking at him through the window. She might say she was fine on her own, but after the two scares she'd had last week, he knew she was nervous being alone. He stopped by the motel front desk long enough to make sure a dog would be okay for their brief stay before heading over to the shelter. On his way, he called the contractor to make sure things were on track with the apartment.

"Sergeant Edwards, I have some good news," the contactor said. "I'm actually a little ahead of schedule on the flooring. Depending on how fast you get the paint colors to me, I can have your apartment finished in about four days."

"How'd you get so far so fast?" Drake asked.

"My son decided he wanted to learn the trade. The flooring was just that snap-together kind, so once I had everything cut to the right measurements, he was able to help lay it. I won't charge extra for him working with me. It's still the same rate I quoted you."

"I appreciate it. And I'll get those paint samples to you tonight."

Drake wrapped up the call and hung up as he was pulling into the parking lot of the animal shelter. He could hear the dogs barking and howling before he'd even opened his truck door. He locked the truck and went inside to see if he could find Shiloh's new best friend. He hoped his trip proved fruitful and he'd be able to find the right dog. Bringing home just anything wasn't acceptable.

He signed in at the front counter and the perky blonde pointed the way to the dog kennels. He hated that they were outside in the heat. The dogs seemed well cared for, but they all looked so sad. He walked up and down both sides several times, but he kept coming back to one kennel in particular. A terrier mix stared at him from the back corner, and its large brown eyes seemed terrified as its poor body trembled. Drake waved for the kennel worker.

"What can you tell me about this one?" he asked.

"His name is Dusty and he's two years old. His owner was a senior woman who passed away, and her family didn't want him."

"So, you don't know how he would be with a baby?"

"I think he would be fine, but I can't say for sure. That holds true for any dog here though." The worker waved at Dusty. "He's really sweet, but all this noise scares him. He's already been neutered and he was up to date on his shots when he came in."

"I'll take him."

The worker nodded and pulled a leash off a nearby post. She opened the kennel and looped the leash around Dusty's neck and led him out. Handing the leash over to Drake, she motioned for him to follow her back to the front desk. It took a few minutes to fill out the adoption forms and pay the fee, and then he was on his way to the pet store. By the time he made it back to the motel, Shiloh was asleep on the bed, her shoes kicked off and her hair in disarray. She looked so damn angelic and his heart ached as he watched her sleep.

The dog squirmed in his arms and he set Dusty down on the bed. He immediately wriggled around Shiloh and licked her on the cheek. Her eyes flew open and she bolted upright in bed. She blinked at him in confusion until the dog yipped. When she saw Dusty, tears gathered in her eyes and she carefully lifted him into her arms, cradling him close.

"You went and bought me a dog?" she asked.

"His owner died and he really needed a new home. I thought maybe we could give him one. The apartment will be done in about four days, if I can get the paint samples to the contractor."

"Does he have a name?" she asked.

"Dusty."

"Hi, Dusty," she cooed at the dog. "You're a good boy, aren't you?"

He yipped again and licked her face. Shiloh laughed and hugged him, looking happier than he'd ever seen her. Best money he'd ever spent. While she was occupied with the dog, he retrieved the stuff from the pet store and put down food and water. Since he wasn't sure how housebroken Dusty was, he'd picked up some puppy pads too and he set one under the counter outside the bathroom.

When he was finished getting everything set up and tossing down a few toys, he kicked off his boots and stretched out next to Shiloh with the dog between them. She rolled onto her side and smiled as she scratched Dusty behind his ears. The dog ran to the foot of the bed, leaped off, and ran a lap around the room. He grabbed one of the stuffed squeaky toys and charged onto the bed again.

"So, you like him?" Drake asked.

"I love him." She wrinkled her nose. "He could use a bath though."

"I'll take care of it. Why don't you find a movie for us to watch while I get this guy cleaned up?" Drake asked as he snagged Dusty.

"I could do it."

"I brought him home this smelly, so I'll clean him. Crap. I meant to call Doctor Thompson while I was out. I wanted to get you in to see him tomorrow. Give me a minute to make a call and then I'll take care of the dog."

As Drake stepped outside so he could talk to the doctor without Dusty making too much noise, he decided he was going to call the vet too. Might as well get both of them checked out before he started his new job and Shiloh returned to work. Having a family was more work than he'd realized, but he was loving every minute of it.

Chapter Twelve

The weekend had flown by, and as the days passed, Shiloh grew more and more attached to Drake. Hell, if she were completely honest with herself, she'd admit that she loved the man. He was always putting her needs first, and she'd thought it was because of the baby, but now she wondered if maybe he felt something for her too. Or maybe it was more that she hoped he did. The way he'd held her hand at the doctor's office… She sighed as she thought about all the intimate moments they'd shared over the past few days.

Shiloh stared at the ultrasound picture Drake had framed for her desk at work. They hadn't been able to tell if they were having a girl or boy because the baby hadn't cooperated, but Doctor Thompson had agreed to try again in a few weeks. She'd gotten a good report, despite the fact she was still a little underweight. Her belly was started to round a little and she looked forward to being able to wear maternity clothes. Drake had been at the appointment with her and had held her hand the entire time. There had been such pride and love in his eyes as he'd stared at the image on the screen.

Charlie had been in the office an hour, but so far, they hadn't discussed the incident from last week. Coming onto the jobsite today, she'd been nervous but not as fearful as she'd thought. The man responsible had been arrested and the foreman had personally escorted her to her desk. He'd introduced her to two other workers, both men he claimed were happily married and would watch over her. It made her feel a little safer, but she wasn't sure she'd ever feel completely at ease around so many men ever again.

Not entirely true. She hadn't felt that way with Drake at the ranch. The cowboys they'd seen were friendly and had never looked at her with anything other than respect. She knew that not all men were pigs, but it was going to be hard not to paint everyone with the same brush for a while. When her boss came out of his office and stopped at the side of her desk, she looked up from the framed picture on the corner of her desk.

"I've been making some calls this morning, and I have a few options for you," Charlie said.

"Options?"

"I would love it if you remained here, but given what happened, I'll understand if you'd prefer to move on. I called a few companies that I know are looking for office help. One has a receptionist opening so you'd only have to answer phones, and the other two have secretary openings so you'd be doing the same thing you do here. They know you'll be out on maternity leave next year, and they were okay with it."

"I don't think I want to leave," Shiloh said. "But I'm nervous about being left alone with the men. What if something happens the next time you go out of town?"

"I discussed it with my foreman, and we just can't guarantee there's not another rotten apple in the bunch, especially with the turnover we have. So, from now on, if I go out of town, I'm giving you time off. Paid time off. I don't leave town very often, so it wouldn't be much of an issue. We could see about having the phones routed to a cell phone you could take with you. And you could always take your laptop home in case you needed to look something up." Charlie shrugged. "It's the best I can come up with right now. If business keeps booming, I'll hire another office worker and then you won't be alone when I'm gone."

"I'd like to stay, if that's okay. I know it doesn't make things very convenient for you…"

Charlie waved away her concern. "I like having

you here, Shiloh. You're a hard worker. If you want to stay, I'm happy to hear it."

He gave her a nod of approval and then stepped into the kitchen. She'd cut back on her caffeine intake, but it didn't mean the smell of brewing coffee didn't still make her mouth water. She wished she could have some, but she instead glared at the bottle of water on her desk. Charlie had apparently bought a case of it and put some in the fridge for her, telling her they were for her and to help herself. She'd noticed a carton of orange juice, too, that hadn't been there the previous week, as well as a bowl of fruit. Between her boss taking care of her at work and Drake taking care of her the rest of the time, she was starting to feel like a spoiled, pampered poodle.

She glanced at the clock and saw that Drake would be coming to get her for lunch in a few hours. He'd asked her to go a little later so he'd have time to shower and change after work. She wondered how his first day was going and wished she could see him in action again. When she'd hooked up a sergeant in the Army, who'd have known she was getting a cowboy in the deal too? Those butt-hugging Wranglers of his were definitely a sight to see, and the hat just made him even sexier.

Shiloh spent the next few hours filing, sorting, and entering data into her laptop. When Drake showed up, hair damp and a polo hugging his broad chest and shoulders, she stared a moment. He gave her that slow, sexy smile of his as he approached her desk, stopping right in front of her.

"See something you like?" he asked with a bit of humor.

"All the time, cowboy."

"Ready for lunch? Or do you need to finish up first?" he asked.

"I'm ready. Anything left on my desk can wait until I return."

Shiloh got her purse from the desk drawer and slipped her hand into Drake's. She'd thought they would go to the diner, since it seemed to be a favorite of his, but he surprised her when he pulled to a stop in front The Roadhouse. He'd ordered out from there on their first night together, but she didn't understand why they were here now. It was a little pricey for lunch, in her opinion.

"Are we celebrating something?" she asked.

"Maybe. Come on. They're holding a table for us."

Shiloh followed him inside, her curiosity piqued further by the secretive smile on the hostess's face. The woman led them to a table in a cozy corner with a single rose in a vase. Shiloh hadn't noticed flowers at the other tables and wondered if Drake had requested it. He pulled out her chair before taking a seat across from her.

"I have some good news," he said.

"You love your new job?" she asked.

"Well, there's that, but not what I was going to say. I talked to the contractor on my way to the motel and he said the apartment is ready. We can go home when you get off work tonight. I'm going to drop you off after lunch and go back to get Dusty and our things."

"That was fast. Do you think everything was done correctly?"

"He had good references so I'm sure the work is fine. What I saw of it when I dropped off the paint samples looked pretty damn good to me. He finished painting last night was just putting all of the furniture and appliances back today."

A waitress came to take their drink order and to leave two menus with them, and then hurried off.

"So, we're eating here to celebrate moving back

into the apartment?" she asked.

"That's part of it."

"Drake, just tell me what's going on. I never did have the patience for guessing games, and pregnancy makes me even less patient."

"Damn, woman. You're going to ruin the surprise if you don't chill out."

She arched a brow but didn't say anything.

When their drinks arrived, the waitress slid a slice of cake in front of her with white frosting and sliced strawberries on top. Shiloh opened her mouth to protest that she hadn't ordered when she saw the look exchanged between Drake and the waitress, and noticed the other wait staff seemed to be watching them with interest. She glanced down at the cake again and gasped when she saw a twinkling diamond ring sticking out of the top.

Drake came around the side of the table and went down on one knee, taking her hand.

"I asked you once before to marry me and you said maybe. I know only a short time has passed since then, but I thought I'd try again, with a ring this time." Drake smiled but looked nervous. "Shiloh, will you marry me?"

"Drake, I…" She glanced around the room before leaning toward him a little. "Are you sure? We don't know each other that well. What if we can't stand living together?"

"Sweetheart, I wouldn't ask if I wasn't sure. I know things have happened fast between us, but I know I don't want to live a day without you by my side. I've never said these words to anyone in my life, other than my parents, but I love you."

Tears misted her eyes. "You love me?"

He nodded.

"But…"

Drake leaned forward and pressed his lips to hers. "I love you, Shiloh. There are no buts, ifs, or maybes. I'm completely crazy about you and can't wait to spend the rest of my life with you. If you'll have me."

Shiloh wrapped her arms around his neck and cried against him. "Yes. I'll marry you."

His arms tightened around her and then he was kissing her again. The restaurant broke out in applause as he pulled away and stood, smiling down at her. Drake wiped the tears from her cheeks, and then he pulled the ring from the cake and wiped the icing off with a napkin before sliding it onto her finger. It was a perfect fit, and she'd never seen a more beautiful ring.

"When did you even have time to go ring shopping?" she asked as he retook his seat.

"I bought it at the antique store. I thought it was more unique than the rings you see in the windows around town. The moment I saw it, I knew it was meant for you. Do you like it?"

"I love it."

"If you don't want the cake," he said, motioning to the piece in front of her, "you don't have to eat it. I just wanted to propose in a slightly different way. I still got down on one knee, but I know how much you love your sweets."

Shiloh looked from the cake to her beautiful ring. Tears misted her eyes again and she hastily wiped them away before taking a bite of the dessert in front of her. By the time their food arrived, she was almost too full to eat it. What she didn't finish, Drake sent back to work with her in case she got hungry before it was time to go home. She hated to return to the office, but she didn't need to miss work on the day her boss returned.

Drake walked her back to her desk and pulled her into his arms for a knee-weakening kiss. When he pulled away, she didn't want to let him go. Shiloh pulled him down for another kiss, not stopping until they were both out of breath and wanting more. A throat cleared behind them and Shiloh turned to see her boss watching them with a smile.

"Why don't you take the rest of the afternoon off, Shiloh?" Charlie asked. "That sparkly bauble on your finger tells me the two of you have something to celebrate."

"He asked me to marry him," she said, smiling broadly.

Charlie chuckled. "And it looks like you said yes. Congratulations to both of you. Now, get out of here. I'll see you at eight tomorrow morning. There's just one more thing I need before you take off."

"What's that?" Shiloh asked.

Charlie tossed her a set of keys. "I need to give you the keys to your company car."

"Company car?" she asked, her brow furrowed. "We don't use company cars."

"Fine. Consider it an early wedding and baby present. I can't have you driving around town in that death trap of yours, especially when your baby arrives. You do enough errands for me that I think it's justified. And before you refuse, you should know it isn't brand new. I got it used, but it has low miles and was a one-owner vehicle. An elderly lady owned it and she's unable to drive anymore so I got it for a steal."

It was on the tip of her tongue to thank him and return the keys, but Drake edged around her to shake Charlie's hand.

"Thank you," Drake said. "I've been trying to figure out how to get her to accept a car, but I knew she'd refuse one if I bought it."

Charlie nodded and shook his hand. "Just do me a

favor."

"Anything," Drake said.

"You get tired of being a cowboy, you come see me for a job. I always have openings, so I don't want the two of you falling on hard times if you don't have to. I've become rather fond of Shiloh since she started working here, and I'd like to help y'all anyway I can." Charlie winked at her. "She's like my pesky younger sister."

Shiloh's heart melted at his words. She remembered him speaking of his sister, and she was honored that he thought of her that way. Hurrying over to him, she hugged him tight and thanked him for the car. Part of her still wanted to refuse it, but deep down she really didn't want to. Even sight unseen, she knew it had to be better than what she'd been driving.

"I'm going to have your old car hauled to the junkyard," Charlie said. "So, anything you need from it should be removed before you leave today."

"It's empty," Shiloh said. "I'll leave the keys to it on my desk, in case the tow truck driver needs them."

"Go enjoy your afternoon," Charlie said, shooing them out.

She dropped her keys on her desk and made sure she had everything. When she got the parking lot, she hit the button on the key fob in her hand and nearly squealed when she saw the cute compact car in the lot that beeped. She didn't know what kind it was, and she didn't care. It looked brand new despite Charlie's words, and she couldn't wait to drive it. Sliding behind the wheel, she followed Drake back to the motel where they gathered Dusty, their things, and then checked out.

At the apartment, Drake made her wait in the car until he had taken everything inside, including Dusty. Then he walked with her up the stairs and covered her eyes before letting her into the apartment. He removed his hand and she gasped at how beautiful it was. She'd chosen a light teal for the living-room walls and an apricot for the kitchen and small dining area. It looked gorgeous with the new wood laminate floors. She explored the rest, checking out their bedroom, which was now a soft green, and the baby room, which was the same yellow Drake had painted it before the contractor had taken over.

The floor in the bathroom was a pretty beige color and made the space seem even larger with the light-lavender walls. She'd been surprised that Drake had allowed the color, but he'd given her free rein over the colors of the rooms. The only thing he'd picked was the flooring, and it was beautiful. She threw her arms around him and hugged him tight.

"I love it. It's the most beautiful place I've ever lived."

"Even though we went with the wood in the kitchen instead of the tile?" he asked.

"I like the wood in there. And is it my imagination or did we get new kitchen appliances too?" she asked.

"They were kind of old. You keep telling me how much you love to cook, so I thought you deserved the proper equipment. That old stove never cooked things evenly, and the fridge was smaller than most. We lost a little cabinet space by adding the dishwasher, but with the baby on the way, I figured you'd appreciate one."

She kissed him. "It's perfect. I may never want to move from here."

"You'll change your mind. Especially when I pull up the website I was checking out the other night. There are tons of house plans on there that we could order to have our place built."

"I just want to enjoy this place for now." She smiled. "But I'll let you know when I'm ready to consider a house."

Drake nibbled along her jaw and down her neck. "What do you say we christen our newly renovated apartment? I even put new bedding in our bedroom."

"Why, Sergeant Edwards. Did you renovate this apartment just so you could get in my pants?"

He winked. "You found me out."

Shiloh shook her head and followed him to the bedroom. As if the man had to spend thousands of dollars to fix up the apartment to get her to sleep with him. All he had to do was wear those tight ass jeans of his and she was putty in his hands … and she was fairly certain he knew it too. Damn smug Texas cowboys.

Drake slowly undressed her and pressed kisses to her slightly rounded belly.

"I think you and this baby are the best things that ever happened to me," he said.

"Who'd have guessed that when the asshole ex stranded me here that I'd end up knocked up on my first night in town? I have to say, despite how scary it was to find out I was pregnant and alone, I wouldn't change a single thing." She narrowed her eyes. "Except that one email."

He gave her a sheepish smile. "How about I send you an email every day for the rest of our lives, or until email is obsolete? And I promise they'll only say the best of things, like how much I love you and can't live without you."

"I'm going to hold you to it."

Drake pulled her into his arms and kissed her until her toes were curling. When she'd landed in Gulch Springs, she'd thought her life was too fucked up to recover. But she'd found great friends, and a man she loved more than anything. Life had never been so sweet before. Shiloh had something she'd never had before. Family. And she was going to hold on with both hands. Her sexy sergeant turned cowboy was everything she'd ever dreamed of, and for once, she was looking forward to what tomorrow would bring.

The End

SERGEANT'S SECRET BABY

EVERNIGHT PUBLISHING ®

www.evernightpublishing.com

www.ingramcontent.com/pod-product-compliance
Lightning Source LLC
Chambersburg PA
CBHW022023170626
46808CB00003B/1036